Missing

Missing

Walter de la Mare

ET REMOTISSIMA PROPE

Modern Voices

Modern Voices
Published by Hesperus Press Limited
4 Rickett Street, London sw6 1ru
www.hesperuspress.com

First published in 1942
First published by Hesperus Press Limited, 2007

Designed and typeset by Fraser Muggeridge studio
Printed in Jordan by the Jordan National Press

ISBN: 1-84391-429-8
ISBN13: 978-1-84391-429-7

Contents

Foreword

In these three tales there is always a first-person narrator, the 'I' voice. In 'Missing' and 'Crewe' the narrator encounters a stranger who tells him a story; in 'The Almond Tree' he hears the story from an old friend. These narrations are not easily described: I think of a lighthouse sweeping the sea with an occulting beam of obscurity and intervals of clarity; I think of a train passing between me and what I'm looking at so that I see the rhythmically interrupted view through its windows; I think of the machine guns of an antique biplane firing between revolutions of the propeller; I think of opening a cupboard door and having the contents of the top shelf fall on me in slow motion.

As often as I've read 'Missing' I still seem to be missing something. The stranger encountered in a London tea shop by our narrator calls himself Bleet. Bleet! Which he does for a very long time during a heat wave. And a drought that has evidently withered his life as well as the grass at his home about seventy miles from London.

Bleet is lonely, has come to London wanting not to be alone; and he's desperate for someone to talk to. His narration is full of pauses and seldom picks up where it left off. Questions and answers in the conversation pass each other at odd angles, missing the point consistently. A Miss Dutton, past her heyday but well preserved – 'It was my house she was missing from', says Bleet – wanted to marry him, that much is clear. Had he encouraged her too much with tinned soups and peaches? Marriage wasn't what he had in mind, we learn while thunder is followed by a torrential rain that has no cooling effect. And what of Maria, Bleet's sister? What actually happened to her and was that connected to Edna Dutton's disappearance? What was the exact nature of the Inquiry? This story is mostly made up of unanswered questions. Perhaps loneliness is the main subject here – the human situation? The missingness of Bleet's sad life that makes him pour his heart out to a stranger in a tea shop until they part with mutual revulsion.

The drought and the heat and Bleet's isolation remain with me; the rain and the thunderstorm that bring no relief; and, insistently, the missingness of this life laid out on the marble table in the tea shop. These seem to me to be the main movers in this mystery. The pathetic sister and the rejected Edna Dutton, standing too close to the edge of it, are swept away with Bleet by the tsunami of missingness. It could happen to anyone.

I don't remember when I first read 'Crewe'; it was a long time ago but that black-leather upholstered first-class waiting room with its dying fire in the winter evening is part of my inner geography – it's always there, a place where I wait from time to time while up trains of thought and down trains of thought rumble past. A little old man in a coat too big for him (the events in his story, we learn, are also too big for him) refers to the 'mysterious and tragic events' on board the *Hesper* on her last voyage. Those who have been discussing those events, he claims, 'had no more notion of what they were talking about than an infant in the cradle'. The reader never learns what actually happened on the *Hesper*. In Longfellow's poem, 'The Wreck of the Hesperus', the skipper's little daughter is found dead and frozen, lashed to a drifting mast after the schooner breaks up on the reef of Norman's Woe. Whatever happened on board the *Hesper* and whatever de la Mare's intention, that little dead girl is now part of this story.

The little old man in the big coat in the first-class waiting room (his name is Blake) was one of the servants at a vicarage 'in the depps of the country' along with a young fellow named George and Menzies, the gardener. Blake caused Menzies to be sacked, which started a chain of events featuring a scarecrow which (who?) is not quite the usual thing but comes and goes at will. What George encounters one night when Blake orders him to go outside the house for a recce is such that Blake is now a very worried man. And in this anxious state he has inhabited the Crewe first-class waiting room in my mind for many years, beaming his story through alternations of obscurity and clarity.

These three tales take us from the heat of summer in 'Missing' to the dead of winter in 'The Almond Tree'. Here the second narrator, 'the Count', recalls his childhood. The characters in his story are archetypal; they might be tarot cards or dancing mechanical figures in a town-hall clock. Perhaps the one that comes out last is hooded and carries a scythe. Before he appears we have The Unknowing Son; The Betrayed Wife; The Beautiful Other Woman; and The Unfaithful Husband. And before these come others, strange and familiar, dancing their allotted round until the mechanism wears out.

Walter de la Mare's poem 'Fare Well' contains these lines:

Look thy last on all things lovely,
Every hour...

Which he does. And always he hears the murmur of the heart of the world, notably in 'The Almond Tree'. The mythical gleams of childhood are counted out like gold coins: *'the steep stairs, the cool apple-scented pantry... the cobbles by the scullery, the well, my old dead raven...'* The treasured memory of 'my old dead raven' in the gold of childhood! The boy Nicholas, his anxious mother, the too-often absent father, and Miss Jane Grey, the boy's siren friend, circle in their clockwork dance as the hours of the guilty secret strike and strike again.

Nicholas as a grown-up recalls 'the first fast-sealed buds upon the almond tree' on a long-gone Valentine's day. Beside this image stands his hard-won knowledge, sheathed, like the winter almond tree, in ice.

– *Russell Hoban, 2007*

Missing

It was the last day of a torrid week in London – the flaming crest of what the newspapers call a *heat wave*. The exhausted inmates of the dazzling, airless streets – plate-glass, white stone, burnished asphalt, incessant roar, din, fume and odour – have the appearance at such times of insects trapped in an oven of a myriad labyrinthine windings and chambers; a glowing brazen maze to torture Christians in. To have a *mind* even remotely resembling it must be Satan's sole privilege!

I had been shopping; or rather, I had been loafing about from one department on to another in one of the huge 'stores' in search of bathing-drawers, a preventative of insect bites, and a good holiday 'shocker', and had retired at last incapable of buying anything – even in a world where pretty well everything except peace of mind can be bought, and sold. The experience had been oppressive and trying to the temper.

Too hot, too irritable even to lunch, I had drifted into a side street, and then into a second-hand bookshop that happened still to be open this idle Saturday afternoon; and having for ninepence acquired a copy of a book on psycho-analysis which I didn't want and should never read, I took refuge in a tea shop.

In spite of the hot-water fountain on the counter it was a degree or two cooler in here, though even the marble-top tables were tepid to the touch. Quiet and drowsy, too. A block of ice surmounted the dinner-wagon by the counter. The white clock face said a quarter to three. Few chairs were now occupied; the midday mellay was over. A heavy slumbrousness muffled the place – the flies were as idle as the waitresses, and the waitresses were as idle as the flies.

I gave my order, and sat back exhausted in a listless vacancy of mind and body. And my dazed eyes, having like the flies little of particular interest to settle on, settled on the only fellow reveller that happened to be sitting within easy reach. At first glimpse there could hardly be a human being you would suppose less likely to attract attention. He was so scrupulously respectable, so entirely innocent of 'atmosphere'. Even a Chelsea psychic would have been compelled to acknowledge that this particular human being had either disposed of his aura or had left it at home. And yet my first glimpses of him had drawn me out of the vacuum into which I had sunk as easily as a cork is drawn out of an empty bottle.

He was sitting at a table to the left, and a little in front of me. The glare from the open door and the gentler light from the cream-blinded shop window picked out his every hair and button. It flooded in on him from the sparkling glittering street, focused him, 'placed' him, arranged him – as if for a portrait in the finest of oils for next year's Academy. Limelight on the actor-manager traversing the blasted heath is mere child's play by comparison.

Obviously he was not 'the complete Londoner' – though that can hardly be said to be a misfortune. On the other hand, there was nothing rural, and only a touch or so of the provincial in his appearance. He wore a neat – an excessively neat – pepper-and-salt tweed suit, the waistcoat cut high and exhibiting the points of a butterfly collar and a triangle of black silk cravat slipped through a gold mourning ring. His ears maybe were a little out of the mode. They had been attached rather high and flat on either side of his conical head with its dark, glossy, silver-speckled hair.

The nose was straight, the nostrils full. They suggested courage of a kind; possibly, even, on occasion, bravado. He looked the kind of man, I mean, it is well to keep out of a corner. But the eyes that were now peering vacantly down that longish nose over a trim but unendearing moustache at the crumbs on his empty plate were too close together. So, at least, it seemed to me. But then I am an admirer of the wide expressive brow – such as our politicians and financiers display. Those eyes at any rate gave this spruce and respectable person just a hint, a glint of the fox. I have never heard, though, that the fox is a dangerous animal even in a corner; only that he has his wits about him and preys on geese – whereas my stranger in the tea shop had been refreshing himself with Osborne biscuits.

It was hot. The air was parched and staled. And heat – unless in Oriental regions – is not conducive to exquisite manners. Far otherwise. I continued to watch this person, indolently speculating whether his little particularities of appearance did not match, or matched too precisely. Those ears and that cravat, for example; or those spruce-moustached nostrils and the glitter of the close-neighbouring eyes. And why had he brought to mind a tightly-packed box with no address on it? He began to be a burden, yet I could not keep my eyes away from him – nor from his hands. They were powerful and hairy, with large knuckles; and now that they were not in use he had placed them on his knees under the dark polished slab of his marble table. Beneath those knees rested his feet (the toes turned in a little) in highly polished boots, with thickish soles and white socks.

There is, I agree, something peculiarly vulgar in thus picking a fellow-creature to pieces. But even Keats so dissected Miss Brawne; and even when he was in love with her: and it was certainly not love at first sight between myself and this stranger.

Whether he knew it or not, he was attaching himself to me; he was making his influence felt. It was odd, then, that he could remain so long unconscious of so condensed a scrutiny. Maybe that particular nerve in him had become atrophied. He looked as if a few other rather important nerves might be atrophied. When he did glance up at me – the waitress having appeared with my tea at the same moment – there was a far-away startled look in his bleak blue-black eyes – as if he had been called back.

Nothing more; and even at that it was much such a look as had been for some little time fixed on the dry biscuit crumbs in his empty plate. He seemed indeed to be a man accustomed to being startled or surprised into vigilance without reason. But having seen me looking at him, he did not hesitate. He carefully took up his hat, his horn-handled and gold-mounted umbrella, and a large rusty scaling leather bag that lay on a chair beside him; rose; and stepping gently over with an almost catlike precision, seated himself in the chair opposite to mine. I continued to pour out my tea.

'You will excuse me troubling you,' he began in a voice that suggested he could sing tenor though he spoke bass, 'but would you kindly tell me the number of the omnibus that goes from here to King's Cross? I am a stranger to this part of London.'

I called after the waitress: 'What is the number of the bus,' I said, 'that goes from here to King's Cross?'

'The number of the bus, you si, that goes from here to King's Cross?'

'Yes,' I said, 'to King's Cross.'

'I'm sure *I* don't know,' she said. 'I'll ask the counter.' And she tripped off in her silk stockings and patent leather shoes.

'The counter will know,' I assured him. He looked at me, moving his lips over his teeth as if either or both for some reason had cause to be uneasy.

'I am something of a stranger to London altogether,' he said, 'and I don't usually come these ways: it's a novelty to me. The omnibuses are very convenient.'

'Don't you? Is it?' I replied. 'Why not?' They were rather point-blank questions (and a gentleman, said Dr Johnson, does not ask questions) but somehow they had slipped out as if at his pressing invitation.

He looked at me, his eyes seeming to draw together into an intenser focus. He was not exactly squinting, but I have noticed a similar effect in the eyes of a dog when its master is about to cry 'Fetch it!'

'You see,' he said, 'I live in the country, and only come to London when I seem to need company – badly, I mean. There's a great contrast between the country and this. All these houses. So many strange faces. It takes one out of oneself.'

I glanced round at the sparsely occupied tables. A cloud apparently had overlaid the sun, for a dull coppery glow was now reflected from the drowsy street. I could even hear the white-faced clock ticking. To congratulate him on his last remark would hardly have been courteous after so harmless an advance. I merely looked at him. What kind of self, I was vaguely speculating, would return into his hospitality when he regained his usual haunts.

'I have a nice little place down there,' he went on, 'but there's not much company. Lonely: especially now. Even a few hours makes all the difference. You would be surprised how friendly a place London can be; the people, I mean. Helpful.'

What can only be described as a faint whinny had sounded in his voice as he uttered that 'helpful'. Was he merely to prove yet another of those unfortunate travellers who have lost the return halves of their railway tickets? Had he marked me down for his prey!

'It is not so much what they say,' he continued, laying his hand on the marble table; 'but just their being about, you know.' I glanced at the heavy ring on its third finger and then at his watch-chain – woven apparently of silk or hair – with little gold rings at intervals along it to secure the plait. His own gaze continued to rest on me with so penetrating, so corkscrew-like an intensity, that I found myself glancing over my shoulder in search of the waitress. She however was now engaged in animated argument with the young lady at the pay-desk.

'Do you live *far* from London?' I ventured.

'About seventy miles,' he replied with an obvious gulp of relief at this impetus to further conversation. 'A nice old house too considering the rent, roomy enough but not too large. Its only drawback in some respects is there's nothing near it – not within call, I mean; and we – I – suffer from the want of a plentiful supply of water. Especially now.'

Why so tactless a remark on this broiling afternoon should have evoked so vivid a picture of a gaunt yellow-brick building perched amid sloping fields parched lint-white with a tropical drought, its garden little more than a display of vegetable anatomies, I cannot say. It was a house of a hideous aspect; but I confess it stirred my interest. Whereupon my stranger, apparently, thought he could safely glance aside; and I could examine him more at leisure. It was not, I have to confess, a taking face. There was a curious hollowness in its appearance. He looked like the shell of a man, or rather, like a hermit crab – that neat pepper-and-salt tweed suit and so on being a kind of second-hand accumulation on his back.

'And of course,' he began again, 'now that I am alone I become' – he turned sharply back on me – 'I become more conscious of it.'

'Of the loneliness?' I suggested.

Vacancy appeared on his face, as if he had for the instant stopped thinking. 'Yes,' he replied, once more transfixing me with those bleak close eyes of his, 'the loneliness. It seems to worsen more and more as the other slips away into the past. But I suppose we most of us have much the same experience; just of that, I mean. And even in London... '

I busied myself with my tea things, having no particular wish at the moment to continue the conversation. But he hadn't any intention of losing his victim as easily as all that.

'There's a case now here in the newspaper this morning,' he went on, his glance wandering off to a copy of the *Daily Mail* that lay on the chair next the one he had just vacated. 'A man not much older than I am – "found dead". Dead. The only occupant of quite a good-sized house, I should judge, at Stoke Newington – though I don't know the place personally. Lived there for years on end without even a charwoman to do for him – to – to work for him. Still even there there was some kind of company, I suppose. He could look out of the window; he could hear people moving about next door. Where I am, there isn't another house in sight, not even a barn, and so far as I can see, what they call Nature doesn't become any the more friendly however long you stay in a place – the birds and that kind of thing. It may get better in time; but it's only a few months ago since I was left quite like this. When my sister died.'

Obviously I was hooked beyond hope of winning free again until this corkscrew persistent creature had had his way with me. The only course seemed to be to get the experience over as quickly as possible. It is not easy, however, to feign an active sympathy; and mention of his dead sister had produced in my mind only a faint reflex image of a dowdy lady no longer young in dingy black. Still, it was an image that proved to be not very far from the actuality.

'Any close companionship like that', I murmured, 'when it is broken is a tragic thing.'

He appeared to have seen no significance in my remark. 'And you see, once there were three of us. Once. It never got into the papers – at least not into the London papers, except just by mention, I mean.' He moistened his lips. 'Did you ever happen to come across a report about a lady, a Miss Dutton, who was "missing"?'

It was a pretty stupid question, for after all, few human beings are so gifted as to be able to recall the names even of the protagonists in genuine *causes célèbres*. To bear in mind every sort of Miss Dutton whose disappearance would be referred to only in news-snippets borrowed by the Metropolitan press from the provincial, would be rather too much of a tax even for those interested in such matters. I sipped my tea and surveyed him as sagaciously as possible; 'Not that I can actually recall,' I said. 'Miss – Dutton? It isn't a very uncommon name. You knew her?'

'Knew her!' he repeated, placing his hands on his knees and sitting stiffly back in his chair, his eyes unflinchingly fixed on mine. 'She lived with us a matter of two years or more. It was us she left. It was my house she was missing from. It caused quite a stir in the neighbourhood. It was the talk of the countryside. There was an Inquiry; and all that.'

'How long ago?'

'Pretty near a year ago. Yes; a year yesterday.'

'Do you mean the Inquiry, or when Miss Dutton disappeared?'

'The Inquiry,' he replied in a muffled fashion, as if a little annoyed at my want of perspicacity. 'The other was – oh, a month or more before that.'

The catechism was becoming a rather laborious way of extracting a story, but somehow its rudiments had begun to interest me. I had nothing to do. To judge from the look of the street, the quicksilver in the thermometer was still edging exquisitely upwards. I detested the thought of emerging into that oven. So apparently did my companion, unless the mere sound of his voice seemed to him better entertainment than, say, the nearest 'picture palace' – where at least one would be out of sight and it would be dark.

'I should have thought,' I began again in a voice as unconcerned as I could manage, 'that living as you do, a stir in the neighbourhood would not much matter, though I agree that the mystery itself must have mattered a good deal more. That of course must have been a great shock to you both.'

'Ay,' he said, with a gleam in his eye, 'but that's just what you Londoners don't seem to understand. You have your newspapers and all that. But in most ways you don't get talked about much.

It's not so in the country. I guarantee you might be living right in the middle of the Yorkshire Moors and yet, if it came to there being anything to keep their tongues wagging, you'd know that your neighbours were talking of you, and what about, for miles around. It gets across – like those black men's drums one hears about in West Africa. As if the mere shock of the thing wasn't enough! What I feel about it is that nowadays people don't seem to show any sympathy, any ordinary feeling with – with those in such circumstances; at least, not country people. Wouldn't you say yourself,' he added, with feline rapidity, 'that if *you* were reported as missing it would be rough luck if nobody cared?'

'I don't quite see what you mean,' I replied. 'I thought you said that the disappearance of your friend made a stir in the neighbourhood.'

'Yes; but they were not thinking so much of *her* as of the cause of it.'

We exchanged a long glance, but without much addition to my own small fund of information. 'But surely,' I ventured, 'that must depend upon where she was supposed to have disappeared *to?*'

'That,' he replied, 'they never knew. We couldn't find out not one iota about it. You've no idea' – he drew his hands down over his face as if to clear away a shadow from his eyes – 'you've no idea. Since she has gone I feel almost sometimes as if she can never have been real. *There*, but not real; if you understand me. I see her; and then the real thing goes again. It never occurred to me, that.'

'The psychologists would tell us something about that.'

'The what?' he asked sharply.

'Oh, those who profess to explain the workings of the mind. After all, we can't definitely say whether that teapot there is real – what it is in itself, I mean. And merely to judge from its looks,' I added, 'one might hope it was a pure illusion.'

He looked hard at the teapot. 'Miss Dutton was a very well-preserved woman for her age,' he said. 'And when I say "not real", it's only in a manner of speaking, I mean. I've got her portrait in the newspaper in my pocket-book. That ought to prove her real enough. I never knew anyone who was more "all there", as they say. She was a good friend to me – I have every reason to remember her. She came along of her own free will – just a chance meeting. In Scarborough, as a matter of fact. And she liked the comforts of a home after all those hotels and boarding houses.'

In the course of these ruminating and mournful remarks – and there was unmistakable 'feeling' in his tones – he was rather privily turning over the contents of an old leather pocket-book with an inelastic black band. He drew out a frayed newspaper cutting and put it down on the table beside the teapot.

'Looking at that, you wouldn't be in much doubt what Miss Dutton was in herself, now, would you? You'd recognize her,' he raised his eyes, 'if she were – if you met her, I mean, in these awful streets? I would myself.'

It was impossible to decide whether this last remark was ironical, triumphant, embittered, or matter-of-fact; so I looked at Miss Dutton. She was evidently a blonde and a well-preserved woman, as my friend had intimated; stoutish, with a plump face, a plump nose, infantile blue eyes, frizzy hair, and she wore (what a few years ago were old-fashioned and are now new-fashioned) long ear-rings.

It was curious what a stabilizing effect the ear-rings produced. They resembled the pole Blondin used to carry as he tripped across his rope over the Niagara Falls. Miss Dutton was looking out of her blurred image with a sort of insouciance, gaiety, 'charm', the charm that photographers aim at but rather seldom convey. Destiny, apparently, casts no retrospective shadow. I defy anybody to have found the faintest hint in that aware, vain, commonplace, good-natured face which would suggest Miss Dutton was ever going to be 'missed' – missed, I mean, in the sense of becoming indiscoverable. In the other sense her friends would no doubt miss her a good deal. But then boarding houses and hotels are the resorts rather of acquaintances than of friends.

The owner of the newspaper snippet was scrutinizing the gay, blurred photograph with as much interest as I was; though to him it was upside-down. There was a queer foolish look on his face, a little feline, perhaps, in its sentimentality.

I pushed back the cutting across the marble table and he carefully reinterred it in his pocket-book. 'I was wondering,' he rambled on as he did so, 'what you might have thought of it – without prejudice, so to speak, if you had come across it – casually-like; in the newspaper, I mean?'

The question was not quite so simple as it sounded. It appeared as if my new acquaintance were in wait for a comment which he himself was eager to supply. And I had nothing much to say.

'It's difficult, you know, to judge from prints in newspapers,' I commented at last. 'They are usually execrable even as caricatures. But she looks, if I may say so, an uncommonly genial woman: feminine – and a practical one, too. Not one, I mean, who would be likely to be missing, except on purpose – of her own choice, that is.' Our eyes met an instant. 'The whole business must have been very disturbing, a great anxiety to you. And, of course, to Miss… to your sister, I mean.'

'My name,' he retorted abruptly, shutting his eyes while a bewildering series of expressions netted themselves on his face, 'my name is Bleet.'

'Miss Bleet,' I added, glancing at the pocket into which the book had by now disappeared, and speculating, too, why so preposterous an *alias* should have occurred to apparently so ready a tongue.

'You were saying "genial",' he added rapidly. 'And that is what they all agreed. Even her only male relative – an uncle, as he called himself, though I can swear she never mentioned him in that or in any other capacity. She hadn't always been what you might call a happy woman, mind you. But they were bound to agree that those two years under my care – in our house – were the happiest in Miss Dutton's life. We made it a real home to her. She had her own rooms and her few bits of furniture – photographs, what-nots and so on, quite private. It's a pretty large house considering the rent – countrified, you know; and there was a sort of a new wing added to it fifty years or more ago. Old-fashioned, of course – open fireplace, no bath, enormous kitchen range – swallows coal by the bushel – and so on – very inconvenient but cheap. And though my sister was not in a position to supervise the house-keeping, there couldn't be a more harmless and affectionate crea-ture. To those, that is, who were kind to her. She'd run away from those who weren't – just run away and hide. I must explain that my poor sister was not quite – was a little weak in her intellects – from her childhood. It was always a great responsibility. But as time went on,' he drew his hand wearily over his face, 'Miss Dutton herself very kindly relieved me of a good deal of that. You said she looked a practical woman; so she was.'

His narrative was becoming steadily more personal, and disconcerting. And yet – such is humanity – it was as steadily intensifying in interest. A menacing rumble of thunder at that moment sounded over the street, and a horse clattered down with its van beyond the open door. My country friend did not appear to have noticed it.

'You never know quite where you are with the ladies,' he suddenly ejaculated, and glanced piercingly up – for at that moment our waitress had drawn near.

'It's a 'Ighteen,' she said, pencil on lip, and looking vacantly from one to the other of us.

'"Ighteen",' echoed her customer sharply; 'what's that? Oh the omnibus. You didn't say what you meant. Thank you.' She hovered on, check-book in hand. 'And please bring me another cup of coffee.' He looked at me as if with the intention of duplicating his order. I shook my head. 'One cup, then, miss; no hurry.'

The waitress withdrew.

'It looks as if rain was coming,' he went on, and as if he were thirsting for it as much as I was. 'As I was saying, you can never be quite sure where you are with women; and, mind you, Miss Dutton was a woman of the world. She had seen a good deal of life – been abroad – Gay Paree, Monte Carlo, and all that. Germany before the war, too. She could read French as free and easy as you could that mennoo there. Paperbound books with pictures on them, and that kind of thing.' He was looking at me, I realized, as if there were no other way of intimating the particular kind of literature he had in mind.

'I used to wonder sometimes what she could find in us, such a lonely place; no company. Though, of course, she was free to ask any friends if she wanted to, and talked of them too when in the mood. Good class, to judge from what she said. What I mean is, she was quite her own mistress. And I must say there could not be more good humour and so on than what she showed my poor sister. At least, until later. She'd talk to her as if conversing; and my sister would sit there by the window, looking back at her and smiling and nodding just as if she were taking it all in. And who knows, perhaps she was. What I mean is, it's possible to have things in your head which you can't quite put into so many words. It's one of the things I look for when I come up to London: the faces that could tell a story though what's behind them can't.'

I nodded.

'I can assure you that before a few weeks were over she had got to be as much at home with us as if we had known her all our lives. Chatty and domesticated, and all that. And using the whole house just as if it belonged to her. All the other arrangements were easy, too. I can say now, and I said it then, that we never once up to then demeaned ourselves to a single word of disagreement about money matters or anything else. A woman like that, who has been all over the continent, isn't likely to go far wrong in that. I agree the terms were on the generous side; but then, you take me, so were the arrangements.

'She asked herself to raise them when she had been with us upwards of twelve months. But I said "No". I said, "A bargain's a bargain, Edna" – we were "Edna" and "William" to one another, by then, and my sister too. She was very kind to my poor sister; got a specialist up all the way from Bath – though for all his prying questions he did nothing, as I knew he wouldn't. You can't take those things so late. Mind you, as I say, the business arrangements were not all on one side. Miss Dutton liked things select and comfortable. She liked things to go smoothly; as we all do, I reckon. She had been accustomed to smart boarding-houses and hotels – that kind of thing. And I did my level best to keep things nice.'

My stranger's face dropped into a rather gloomy expression, as if poor humanity had sometimes to resign itself to things a little less agreeable than the merely smooth and nice. He laid down his spoon, which he had been using with some vigour, and sipped his coffee.

'What I was going to explain,' he went on, rubbing at his moustache, 'is that everything was going perfectly easy – just like clockwork, when the servant question came up. My house, you see, is on what you may call the large side. It's old in parts, too. Up to then we had had a very satisfactory woman – roughish but willing. She was the wife, or what you might just as well call the widow, of a sailor. I mean he was one of the kind that has a ditto in every port, you know. She was glad of the place, glad to be where her husband couldn't find her, even though the stipulation was that her wages should be permanent. That system of raising by driblets always leads to discontent. And I must say she was a fair tyrant for work.

'Besides her, there was a help from the village – precious little good *she* was. Slummocky – and *stupid!* Still, we had got on pretty well up to then, up to Miss Dutton's time, and for some months after. But cooking for three mouths is a different thing to two. Besides, Miss Dutton liked her meals dainty-like: a bit of fish, or soup occasionally, toast-rack, tantalus, serviettes on the table – that kind of thing. But all that came on gradual-like – the thin edge of the wedge; until at last, well, "exacting" wasn't in it.

'And I must say,' he turned his wandering eye once more on mine, 'I must say, she had a way of addressing menials which sometimes set even my teeth on edge. She was a lady, mind you – though what *that* is when the breath is out of your body it's not so easy to say. And she had the lady's way with them – those continental hotels, I suppose. All very well in a large establishment where one works up against another and you can call them names behind their backs. But our house wasn't an establishment. It wouldn't do there: not in the long run, even if you had an angel for a general, and a cook to match.

'Mind you, as I say, Miss Dutton was always niceness itself to my poor sister: never a hard word or a contemptuous look – not to her face nor behind her back, not up to then. I wouldn't have tolerated it either. And you know what talking to a party that can only just sit, hands in lap, and gape back at you means, or maybe a word now and then that doesn't seem to have anything to do with what you've been saying. It's a great affliction. But servants were another matter. Miss Dutton couldn't demean herself to them. She lived in another world. It was, "Do this"; and "Why isn't it done?" – all in a breath. I smoothed things over, though they got steadily worse and worse, for weeks, and weeks, ay, months. It wore me to a shadow.

'And one day the woman – Bridget was her name – Irish, you know – she flared up in earnest and gave her, as they say, as good as she got. I wasn't there at the time. But I heard afterwards all that passed, and three times over – on the one side at least. I had been into the town in the runabout. And when I came home, Mrs Tantrums had packed up her box, got a gig from the farm, and was gone for good. It did me a world of harm, that did.

'Pretty well upset, I was too, as you can imagine. I said to Miss Dutton, "Edna," I said, "all I am saying is, was it necessary to go to such extremes? Not," I said, "mind you, Edna, that she was all sugar and honey even to me. I knew the wrong side of her mouth years before *you* appeared on the scene. What you've got to do with such people is – to manage – be firm, keep 'em low, but manage. It isn't commonsense to cut off your tongue to spite your teeth. She's a woman, and Irish at that," I said, "and you know what to expect of them."

'I was vexed, that's a fact, and perhaps I spoke rather more sharply than need have been. But we were good friends by that time: and if honest give-and-take isn't possible between friends, where are you? I ask you. There was by that time too, nothing left over-private between us, either. I advised her about her investments and so on, though I took precious good care not to be personally involved. Not a finger stirring unless she volunteered it first. That all came out too. But it was nothing to do with me, now, was it, as man to man, if the good lady took a fancy into her head to see that my poor sister was not left to what's called the tender mercies of this world after my death?

'And yet, believe me, they fixed on that, like leeches. My hell, they did! At the Inquiry, I mean. And I don't see how much further their decency could have gone if they had called it an Inquest; and… '

Yet another low (almost gruff) volley of thunder interrupted his discourse. He left the sentence in the air; his mouth ajar. I have never met anyone that made such active use of his chin in conversation, by the way, as Mr Bleet did. It must have been exceedingly fatiguing. I fancy he mistook just then the expression on my face for one of inquiry. He leant forward, pushing down towards me that long hairy finger on the marble table-top.

'When I say "tender mercies",' he explained, 'I don't mean that my sister would have been left penniless, even if Miss Dutton or nobody like her had come into the house. There was money of my own too, though, owing to what I need not explain' – he half swallowed the words – 'not much.' He broke off. 'It seems as if we are in for a bit of a thunderstorm. But I'd sooner it was here than down my way. When you're alone in the house you seem to notice the noise more.'

'I fancy it won't be much,' I assured him. 'It will clear the air.'

His eyes opened as if in astonishment that any mere act of nature could bring such consolation.

'You were saying,' I exclaimed, 'that you lost your maid?' He glanced up sharply. 'Though of course,' I added hastily, 'you mustn't let me intrude on your private affairs.'

'Not at all; oh, not at all,' he interrupted with relief. 'I thought you said, "lost my head". Not at all. It makes all the difference to me – I can assure you, to be able to go over it like this. Friendly like. To get a listener who has not been fed up on all that gossip and slander. It takes some living down, too. Nothing satisfies them: nothing. From one week's end to another you can't tell where they'll unearth themselves next.'

It was becoming difficult to prevent a steadily growing distaste for my companion from showing itself in my face. But then self-pity is seldom ingratiating. Fortunately the light where we sat was by now little better than dusk. Indeed, to judge from the growing gloom in our tea shop, the heavens at this moment were far from gracious. I determined to wait till the rain was over. Besides, though my stranger himself was scarcely winning company, and his matter was not much above the sensational newspaper order, the mere zigzagging of his narrative was interesting. Its technique, I mean, reminded me of the definition of a crab: 'The crab is a little red animal that walks backwards.'

'The fact is,' he went on, 'on that occasion – I mean about the servant – Miss Dutton and I had words. I own it. Not that she resented my taking the thing up in a perfectly open and friendly way. She knew she had put me in a fair quandary. But my own private opinion is that when you are talking to a woman it's best not to bring in remarks about the sex in general. A woman is herself or nothing, if you follow me. What she thinks is no more than another skin. Keep her sex out of it, and she'll be reasonable. But no further. As a matter of fact, I never argue with ladies. But I soon smoothed that over. It was only a passing cloud. And I must say, considering what a lady she *was*, she took the discomforts of having nothing but a good-for-nothing slattern in the house very generously, all things considered.

'Mind you, I worked *myself*, fit for any couple of female servants: washed up dishes, laid the table, kept the little knick-knacks going. Ay, and I'd go into the town to fetch her out little delicacies: tinned soups and peaches, and such like; anything she might have a taste to. And I taught her to use the runabout for herself, though to hear her changing gear was like staring ruin in the face. A gallon of petrol to a hank of crimson silk – that kind of thing. Believe me, she'd go all those miles for a shampoo-powder, or to have tea at a tea shop – though you can't beat raw new-laid eggs and them on the premises. They got to know her there. She was a rare one for the fashions:

scarves and motor-veils, and that kind of thing. But I never demurred. It wasn't for me to make objections, particularly as she'd do a little shopping on the housekeeping side as well, now and then. Though, mind you, she knew sixpence from a shilling, and particularly towards the last.

'What was the worst hindrance was that my poor sister seemed to have somehow come to know there were difficulties in the house. I mean that there had begun to be. You don't know how they do it; but they do. And it doesn't add to your patience, I grant, when what you have done at one moment is done wrong over again the next. But she meant well, poor creature: and scolding at her only made things worse. Still, we got along happily enough for a time, until' – he paused once more with mouth ajar – 'until Miss Dutton took it into her head to let matters come to a crisis. Now judging from that newspaper cutting I showed you, what would you take the lady's age to be? Allowing, as you might say, for all that golden hair?'

It was an indelicate question. Though why the mere fact that Miss Dutton was now missing should intensify its indelicacy, it is not easy to say.

'Happiness makes one look younger than one really is,' I suggested.

He gaped at me, as if in wonderment that in a world of woe he himself was not possessed of a white beard as long as your arm.

'"Happiness?"', he echoed.

'Yes, happiness.'

'Well, what I mean is, you wouldn't say she was in the filly class; now, would you? High-spirited, easy-going, and all that; silly, too, at times: but no longer young. Not in her heyday, I mean.'

I pushed my empty cup aside and looked at him. But he looked back at me without flinching, as if indeed it was a pleasant experience to be sharing with a stranger sentiments so naïve regarding 'the fair sex'.

'Mind you, I don't profess to be a young man either. But I can assure you on my word of honour, that what she said to me that evening – I was doing chores in the kitchen at the time, and she was there too, arranging flowers in a vause for supper; she had a dainty taste in flowers – well, she asked me why I was so unkind to her, so unresponsive, and – it came on me like a thunderbolt.'

As if positively for exemplification, a violent clap of thunder at that moment resounded overhead. The glasses and crockery around us softly tinkled in sympathy. We listened in silence to its reverberations dying away across the chimney-tops; though my companion seemed to be taking them in through his mouth rather than through his ears. His cheek paled a little.

'That's what she asked me, I say. And I can tell you it took me on the raw. It was my turn to flare up. We had words again: nothing much, only a storm in a tea-cup.' Instead of smiling at this metaphor in the circumstances, he seemed astonished, almost shocked, at its aptitude. But he pushed on boldly.

'And then after I had smoothed things over again, she put her cards on the table. Leap Year, and all that tomfoolery, not a bit of it! She was in dead earnest. She told me what I had guessed already, that she had scarcely a friend in the world. Never a word, mind you, of the Colonel – interloping old Pepper-face! She assured me, as I say, she hadn't not only a single relative, but hardly a friend; that she was, as you might say, alone in life, and – well, that her sentiments had become engaged. In honour bound I wouldn't have breathed this to a living soul who knew the parties; but to a stranger, if I may say so, it isn't quite the same thing. What she said was – in the kitchen there, and me in an apron, mind you, tied round me – doing chores – she said – well, in short, that she wanted to make a match of it. She had taken a fancy to me, and was I agreeable.' There was no vanity in his face; only a stark un-philosophical astonishment. He seemed to think that to explain all is to forgive all; and was awaiting my concurrence.

'You mean she proposed marriage,' I interrupted him with needless pedantry, and at once, but too late, wished the word back. For vestiges of our conversation had evidently reached the counter. Our waitress, still nibbling her pencil, was gazing steadily in our direction. And for some obscure reason this heat that we were sharing with the world at large, combined with this preposterous farrago, was now irritating me almost beyond endurance. The fellow's complacency was incredible.

I beckoned to the young woman. 'You said this gentleman's bus to King's Cross was an Eighteen, didn't you?'

'Yes, 'Ighteen,' she repeated.

'Then would you please bring him an ice.'

Mr Bleet gazed at me in stupefaction; a thick colour had mounted into his face. 'You don't mean to say,' he spluttered, 'that *I* made any such mention of such a thing. I'm sure I never noticed it.'

My impulse had been nothing more than a protest against my own boredom and fatigue; but the way he had taken it filled me with shame. What could the creature's state of mind be like if his memory was as untrustworthy as that? The waitress retired.

'It's so devilishly hot in here,' I explained. 'And even talking is fatiguing in this weather.'

'Ay,' he said in a low voice. 'It is. But you aren't having one yourself?'

'No, thank you,' I said, 'I daren't. I can't take ices. Indigestion – it's a miserable handicap… You were saying that at the time of Miss Dutton's proposal, you were in the kitchen.'

There was a pause. He sat looking foolishly at the little glass dishful of ice-cream: as surprising a phenomenon apparently as to an explorer from the torrid zone earth's northern snows must first appear. There was a look upon his face as if he had been 'hurt', as if, like a child, at another harsh word he might burst out crying.

'I hardly know that it's worth repeating,' he said at last lamely. His fine resonant voice had lost its tone. 'I suppose she intended it kindly enough. And I wouldn't say I hadn't suspected which way the wind was blowing: Willie this, and Willie that. I've always been William to them that know me, except Bill at school. But it was always Willie with her; and a languishing look to match. Still, I never expected what came after that. It took me aback.

'There she was, hanging on my every word, looking volumes, and me not knowing what to say. In a way too, I was attached to her. There were two sides to her, I allow that.' He turned away but not, it seemed, in order to see the less conspicuous side more clearly. 'I asked her to let me think things over, and I said it as any gentleman would. "Let me think it over, Edna," I said. "You do me honour," I said. Her hand was on my arm. She was looking at me. God being my witness, I tried to spare her feelings. I eased it over, meaning it all for the best. You see that little prospect had no more than occurred to me. Married life wasn't what I was after. I shouldn't be as old as I am now – and unmarried, I mean – if that had been so. It was uncomfortable to see her carrying on like that: too early. But things having come to such a pass, well, as you might say, we glided into an understanding at last. And with what result? Why... she made it an occasion for putting her foot down all the way round. And hadn't I known it of old?'

He looked at me searchingly, with those dog-bright eyes, those high-set ears, as if to discover where precisely I now was in relation to his confidences.

'She took the reins, as they say. All in good temper for the most part; but there was no mistaking it. Mistress first and Mrs after, in a manner of speaking. But when it came to speaking sharply to my poor sister on a matter which you wouldn't expect even a full-witted person to be necessarily very quick about at the uptake – I began to suspect I had made a mistake. I knew it then: but forewarned isn't always forearmed. And mistakes are easier to make than to put right. It had gone too far... '

'If you really don't want that ice, I can easily ask the waitress to take it away,' I assured him, if only to bring back that wandering empty eye from the reverie into which he seemed to have fallen. Or was it that he was merely absorbed in the picture of the rain-drenched street that was reflected in the looking-glass behind my chair?

'Thank you,' he said, taking up the spoon.

'And Miss Dutton left you at last. Did she tell you she had any intention of going?'

'Never,' he asseverated. 'Not a word. No, not a single word. And if you *can't* explain it, well then, why go on trying? I say. Not at this late day. But you might as well argue with a stone wall. The heat had come by then. Last summer, you know: the drought. Not the great drought, I mean – but round our parts in particular. The whole place was dried up to a tinder; cracks in the clay; weeds dying; birds gone. Even the trees flagging: and the oaks half eaten up by caterpillars already. Meantime, I don't know how it was – unless, perhaps, the heat – but there had been another quarrel. They never got *that* out of me at the Inquiry, though; I can tell you. And that was patched up, too. I apologized because she insisted. But she had hurt me; she had hurt my feelings. And I couldn't see that marriage was going to be a very practical experiment on those lines. But she came round; and considering what an easy woman of the world she looks like in that photograph, you wouldn't have guessed, would you, that crying, weeping, I mean, was much in her way? I found that out, too. Fatiguing.

'And it didn't suit her, either. But she was what they call a woman made for affection. And I mean by *that*,' he broke in emphatically, 'she liked to monopolize. She wasn't a sharer. We were badly in want of a servant ourselves by that time, as you may imagine. Going from bad to worse, and me with a poisoned thumb, opening tins. But *she* was in want of a servant still more. She wanted me. Husbands often are nothing much better. What's more, I don't wish to say anything against the – against her now; but for the life of me I can't see any reason why she should have gone so far as to insult me. And not a week since we were like birds on one roost. To insult me, mind you, with my poor sister there, listening by!

'But I had learned a bit by then. I held my tongue, though there was a plenty of things to say in reply if I could have demeaned myself to utter them. Plenty. I just went on looking out of the window, easing myself with my foot – we were in the drawing-room at the time – and the very sight of the dried-up grass and the dead vegetables, and the sun pouring down out of the sky like lava from a volcano would have been enough in themselves to finish off most people's self-restraint. But as I say, I just stood there thinking of what I might have said, but saying nothing – just let her rant on.

'Why, for instance, do you suppose she had made out weeks before that her investments were bringing in twice as much as they really did? Why all that stuff about Monte Carlo and the lady from America when it was only Boulogne and what they call a *pension*, which in plain English is nothing more than lodgings? Mind you,' he said, as if to intercept the remark I had no intention of making, 'mind you. I agree there *was* a competence, and I agree that apart from a silly legacy to the Home for Cats and Dogs and that Belgian knacker trade, she had left all there was to leave to my sister – and long before what I told you about just now. I saw that in black and white. It was my duty.

That was all settled. On the other hand, how was I to know that she wouldn't change her mind; that she hadn't been paving the way, as you may call it? And why had she deliberately deceived me? I thought it then, and I think it now, more than ever – considering what I have been through. It wasn't treating me fairly, and particularly before she was in a position when things couldn't be altered, so to speak, as between husband and wife. Stretch it too far, and… '

Owing to the noise of the rain – and possibly in part to his grammar – it was only with difficulty that I could now follow what the creature was mumbling. I found my attention wandering. A miniature Niagara at least eighteen inches wide was at this moment foaming along the granite gutter while the rain in the middle of the street as it rebounded above the smoking asphalt was lifting into the air an exquisite mist of spray. I watched it enthralled; it was sweet as the sight of palm-trees to my tired hot eyes, and its roar and motion lulled me for a moment or two into a kind of hypnotic trance. When I came back to myself and my trivial surroundings, I found my companion eyeing me as if he had eagerly taken advantage of these moments of oblivion.

'That's the real thing,' he said, as if to humour me, beckoning with his thumb over his shoulder. 'That rain. But it's waste on only stones.' He eyed it pensively, turning his head completely round on his narrow shoulders to do so. But only for a moment. He returned to the business in hand as promptly as if we gossipers had been called to order by the Chairman of a Committee.

'Now it says in that report there, which you have just been reading, that Miss Dutton had not been seen after she left Crowstairs that afternoon of the third of July. That's what it says – in so much print. And I say that's a lie. As it came out later on. And it doesn't make it any truer being in print. It's inaccurate – proved so. But perhaps I ought to tell you first exactly how the whole thing came about. Things get so confused in memory.' Once more he wearily drew his hand over his face as if to obliterate even the memory itself. 'But – quite apart from the others – it's a relief to get things clearer even in one's own mind. The fact is, the whole thing was over between us a day or two before. As I say, after the last little upset which I told you about, things were smoothed out again as usual. At least on her side, though there was precious little in which I was really myself at fault. But my own belief is that she was an hysterical woman. What I mean is, she didn't need anything to make a fuss about; to fire up over. No foundation except just her own mood and feelings. I never was what they call a demonstrative person; it isn't in our family. My father himself was a schoolmasterish kind of man. "It hurts me more than it hurts you"; that kind of man. And up to the age of ten I can honestly say that I never once heard my mother answer him back. She felt it, mind you. He thrashed me little short of savage at times. She'd look on, crying; but she kept herself in. She knew it only made matters worse; and she died when I was twelve.

'Well, what I think is this – that Miss Dutton made a mistake about me. She liked comfort. Breakfast in bed; slippers at night; hot water to wash in; that kind of thing. I'll go further: she was meant for luxury. You could see it in her habits. If she had been twice as well off, she'd have wanted three times as many luxuries: lady's maid, evening dress, tea-gowns, music in the drawing-room – that sort of thing. And maybe it only irritated her when she found that I could keep myself in and just look calm, whatever she did or said. Hesitate to say whatever came into her mind? – not she! – true or untrue. Nor actual physical violence, either. Why months before, she threw a vause full of flowers at me: snowdrops.'

The expression on his face suddenly became fixed, as if at an unexpected recollection.

'I am not suggesting,' he testified earnestly, 'considering – considering what came after, that I bear her any grudge or malice on account of all that. All I mean is that I was pressed and pushed on to a point that some would say was beyond human endurance. Maybe it was. But what I say is, let', his voice trembled, 'bygones be bygones. I will say no more of that. My point is that Miss Dutton, after all, was to be, as they say, a bird of passage. There had been a final flare up and all was over between us. Insult on insult she heaped on me. And my poor sister there, in her shabby old black dress, peering out at us, from between her fingers, trembling in the corner like a dumb animal. She had called her in.

'And me at my wits' end, what with the servant trouble and the most cantankerous and unreasonable lot of tradespeople you could lay hands on, north or south. I can tell you, I was pretty hard pressed. They dragged all that up at the Inquiry. Oh, yes, bless you. Trust 'em for that. Once it's men against man, then look to it. Not a *public* Inquiry, mind you. No call for that. And I *will* say the police, though pressing, and leaving no stone unturned in a manner of speaking, were gentlemen by compar- ison. But such things leak out. You can't keep a penny-a-liner from gabbing, and even if there had been nothing worse to it they'd have made my life a hell upon earth.'

'Nothing worse to it? How do you mean?'

His glance for the instant was entirely vacant of thought. 'I mean,' he said stubbornly, after a moment's hesitation, 'the hurt to my private feelings. That's what I mean. I can hear her now. And the first thing I felt after it was all over, was nothing but relief. We couldn't have hit it off together, not for long: not after the first few weeks, anyhow. Better, I say, wash your hands of the whole thing. I grant you her decision had left me in a nasty pickle. As a matter of fact, she was to go in a week, and me to clear up the mess. Bills all over the place – fresh butter, mind you, olives, wine, tinned mock turtle – that kind of thing; and all down to my account. What I feel is, she oughtn't to have kept on at me like that right up to the last. Wouldn't you have thought, considering all things, any woman with an ounce of commonsense – not to speak of common caution – would have let sleeping dogs lie?'

He was waiting for an answer.

'What did her uncle, the Colonel, say to that?'

'Oh, him,' he intimated with an incredible sneer. 'In the Volunteers! I was speaking as man to man.'

'And she didn't even wait the two or three days, then?'

'It was the 3rd of July,' he repeated. 'After tidying things up for the day – and by that time, mind you, every drop of water had to be brought in buckets across the burnt-up fields from a drying-up pond half a mile away. But it was done. I did it. After finishing, I say, all the rest of the morning chores, I was sitting there thinking of getting a snack of lunch and then what to do next, when I heard a cough – her door had opened; and then her footstep on the stairs – slippers.' He held up that forefinger as if at an auction, and he was speaking with extreme deliberation as if, with eyes and senses fixed on the scene, he were intent to give me the exactest of records in the clearest of terms. 'And I said to myself, "She's coming! and it's all to begin again!" I said it; I knew it. "And face it out?... then – me?"' He shook his head a little like a cat tasting water, but the eyes he showed me were like the glazed windows of an empty shop. 'No, I made myself scarce. I said to myself: "Better keep your distance. Make yourself scarce; keep out of it." And heaven help me I had been doing my best to forget what had passed the night before and to face what was to come. And so – I went out.

'It was early afternoon: sultry, like now. And I wandered about the fields. I must have gone miles and never met a soul. But if you ask me to say where, then all I can say is: Isn't one field the living image of another? And what do you see when your mind isn't there? All round Winstock way – lanes, hedges, cornfields, turnips – tramp and tramp and tramp. And it was not until about seven o'clock that evening that I got back again. Time for supper. I got out the crockery and – and raked out the fire. No sign of nobody, nor of my sister either – though there was nothing in that: she had a habit of sitting up at her bedroom window, and looking out, just with her hands in her lap. And the house as still as a – as still as a church.

'I loafed about a bit in the kitchen. Call *her?* Well, hardly! There was plenty to do. As usual. The supper, and all that. The village woman had left about eleven that morning – toothache. She owned to it. Not that that put me about. I can cook a boiled egg and a potato well enough for most Christians. But hot meals – meals for – well, anyhow, there was nothing hot that evening. It was about seven-thirty by then, I suppose; and I was beginning to wonder. Then I thought I'd go out in the yard and have a look at the runabout – an old Ford, you know – I hadn't had time then for weeks to keep it decent. When I got to the shed, there was a strange cat eating up some fish-bones; and when I looked in, it was gone.'

'You mean the Ford?'

'Yes, the Ford. There wasn't a sign of it. That froze me up, I can tell you, for there had been gipsies about a day or two before. I rushed into the house and called out up the stairs, "Edna! Edna! Are you there? The Ford's gone." No answer. I can tell you I was just like a frenzied man. I looked in the drawing-room – teapot and cup on a tray but empty: just sunshine streaming in as if nothing had happened. Then I looked into her little parlour: boudoir, she called it. Nothing doing. Then I went upstairs and tapped on her bedroom door. "Miss Dutton," I said, "have you seen anything of the Ford? It's gone." And then I looked in. That was the queer thing about it.

They all said that. That it never occurred to me, I mean, that she was not in the car herself. But what I say is – how can you think of everything before you say it, and wasn't it I myself that *said* I had said it?

'Anyhow, I looked in: I suppose a man can do *that* in his own house and his car gone from under his very nose! And believe me, the sight inside was shocking. I'm a great stickler myself for law and order, for neatness, I mean. I had noticed it before: it irritated me. In spite of all her finery, she was never what you would call a tidy woman. But that room beat everything. Drawers flung open, dresses hugger-mugger, slippers, bags, bead-work, boxes, gimcracks all over the place. But not a sign of her. I looked – everywhere. She wasn't there, right enough. Not – not a sign of her. She was gone. And – and I have never seen her since.'

The rain was over, and the long sigh he uttered seemed to fill the whole tea shop as if it were a faint echo of the storm which had ceased as suddenly as it had begun. The sun was wanly shining again, gilding the street.

'You at once guessed, I suppose, the house had been broken into, while you were out?'

He kept his eyes firmly on mine. 'Yes,' he said. 'That's what I thought – at first.'

'But then, I think you said a minute or two ago that Miss Dutton *was* actually seen again?'

He nodded. 'That's just it,' he said, as if with incredulous lucidity. 'So you see, the other couldn't have been. The facts were against it. She was seen that very evening,' he said, 'and driving my Ford. By more than one, too. Our butcher happened to be outside his shop door; no friend of mine either. It was a Saturday, cutting up pieces for the 4d. and 6d. trays, and he saw her going by: saw the number too. It was all but broad daylight, though it's a narrow street. It was about seven then, he said, because he had only just wound his clock. There she was; and a good pace too. And who could be surprised if she looked a bit unusual in appearance? It's exactly what you'd expect. You don't bolt out of a house you have lived in comfortable for two or three years as neat as a new pin.'

'What was wrong with her?'

'Oh, the man was nothing better than a fool, though promptitude itself when it came to asking a good customer to settle up. He said he'd have hardly recognized her. There, in my car, mind you, and all but broad daylight.'

'But surely,' I said as naturally as possible, 'even if it is difficult sometimes to trace a human being, it is not so easy to dispose of a car. Wasn't that ever found?'

He smiled at me, and in a more friendly way than I should have deemed possible in a face so naturally inexpressive.

'You've hit the very nail on the head,' he assented. 'They did find the car – on the Monday morning. In fact it was found on the Sunday by a young fellow out with his sweetheart, but they thought it was just waiting – picking flowers, or something. It had been left inside a fir-copse about a couple of hundred yards from a railway station, a mile or so out of the town.'

'Just a countryfied little railway station, I suppose? Had the porter or anybody noticed a lady?'

'Countryfied – ay, maybe: but the platform crowded with people going to and fro for their week's marketing, besides a garden party from the Rectory.'

'The platform going into the town?'

'Yes, that's it,' said my friend. 'Covering her tracks.'

At that moment I noticed one of our waitress's bright-red 'Eighteens' whirling past the tea shop door. It vanished.

'She had had a letter that morning – postmark Chicago,' the now far-too-familiar voice edged on industriously. 'The postman noticed it, being foreign. It's my belief *that* caused it. But mind you, apart from that, though I'm not, and never was, complaining, she'd treated me, well – ' But he left the sentence unfinished while he clumsily pushed about with his spoon in the attempt to rescue a fly that had strayed in too far in pursuit of his sweet cold coffee. He was breathing gently on the hapless insect.

'And I suppose, by that time, you had given the alarm?'

'Given the alarm?' he repeated. 'Why?'

The sudden frigidity of his tone confused me a little. 'Why,' I said, 'not finding Miss Dutton in the house, didn't you let anybody know?'

'Now my dear sir,' he said, 'I ask you. How was I to know what Miss Dutton was after? I wasn't Miss Dutton's keeper; she was perfectly at liberty to do what she pleased, to come and go. How was I to know what she had taken into her head? Why, I thought for a bit it was a friendly action considering all things, that she should have borrowed the car. Mind you, I don't say I wasn't disturbed as well, her not leaving a word of explanation, as she had done once before – pinned a bit of paper to the kitchen table – "Yours with love, Edna" – that sort of thing. Though that was when everything was going smooth and pleasant. What I did first was to go off to a cottage down the lane and inquire there. All out, except the daughter in the washhouse. Not a sight or sound of car or Miss Dutton, though she did recollect the honk of a horn sounding. "Was it my horn?" I asked. But they're not very observant, that kind of young woman. Silly-like. Besides, she wasn't much more than a child.'

'And your sister: where actually was she, after all?'

He looked at me as if once more in compliment of my sagacity.

'That, I take it – to find and question *her*, I mean, was a matter of course. I went up to her room, opened the door, and I can hear myself actually saying it now: "Have you seen anything of Edna, Maria?"

'It was very quiet in her room – stuffy, too, and for the moment I thought she wasn't there; and then I saw her – I detected her there – crouching in the farthest corner out of the light. I saw her white face turn round, it must have been covered up. "Where's Edna, Maria?" I repeated. She shook her head at me, sitting there beyond the window. I could scarcely see her. And you don't seem to have realized that any kind of direct or sudden question always confused her. It didn't seem she understood what I was saying. In my belief it was nothing short of brutal the way they put her through it. I mean that Colonel, as he calls himself. Over and over and over again.

'Well, we weren't in any mood for food, as you may guess, when eight, nine, went by – and no sign of her. At last it was no use waiting any longer; but just to make sure, I went over to the farm two miles or so away – a little off the road, too, she must have taken to the town. We were still pretty friendly there. It was about half-past nine, I suppose, and they had all gone to bed. The dog yelled at me as if it was full moon and he had never seen me before. I threw a handful of gravel up at the old man's window, and I must say, considering all things, he kept his temper pretty well. Specially as he had seen nothing. Nothing whatever, he said.

'"Well," I said, speaking up at him, and they were my very words, "I should like to know what's become of her." He didn't seem to be as anxious as I was – thought she'd turn up next morning. "That kind of woman knows best what she's about," he said. So I went home and went to bed, feeling very uneasy. I didn't like the feel of it, you understand. And I suppose it must have been about three or four in the morning when I heard a noise in the house.'

'You thought she had come back?'

'What?' he said.

'I say, you thought she had come back?'

'Yes, of course. Oh yes. And I looked out of my bedroom door over the banisters. By that time there was a bit of moonlight showing, striking down on the plaster and oilcloth. It was my sister, with an old skirt thrown over her nightgown. She was as white as a sheet, and shivering.

'"Where have you been, Maria?" I asked her in as gentle a voice as I could make it. The curious thing is, she understood me perfectly well. I mean she answered at once, because often I think really and truly she did understand, only that she couldn't as quickly as most people collect her wits as they say.

'She said, mumbling her words, she had been looking for her.

'"Looking for who?" I said, just to see if she had taken me right.

'"For her," she said.

'"For Edna?" I asked. "And why should you be looking for Edna this time of night?" I spoke a little more sternly.

'She looked at me, and the tears began to roll down her face.

'"For God's sake, Maria, why are you crying?" I said.

'"Oh," she said, "she's gone. And she won't come back now."

'I put my arm round her and drew her down on to the stairs. "Compose yourself," I said to her, "don't shiver and shake like that." I forgot she had been standing barefoot on the cold oilcloth. "What do you mean, Gone? Don't take on so. Who's to know she won't come back safe and sound?" I am giving you the words just as they came out of our mouths.

'"Oh," she said, "William, you know better than me – I won't say anything more. Gone. And never knowing that I hadn't forgotten how kind she was to me!"

'"Kind, my girl!" I said. "Kind! In good part, maybe," I said, "but not surely after what she said to you that day?"

'But I could get nothing more out of her. She shrank up moaning and sobbing. She had lost herself again, her hair all draggled over her eyes, and she kept her face averted from me, and her shoulders were all humped, shaking under my hands – you know what women are. So I led her off to her room and made her as comfortable as I could. But all through the night I could hear her afterwards when I went to listen, and talking too.

'You can tell I was by now in a pretty state myself. That was a long night for me. And what do you think: when I repeated that conversation to the Colonel, and the Inspector himself standing by, he as good as told me he didn't believe me. "Friendly questions"! I could have wrung his nose. But then by that time my poor sister couldn't put two words together, he bawled at her so; until even the Inspector said it was not fair on her, and that she wouldn't be any use, anyhow, whatever happened.'

Once again there fell a pause in my stranger's disjointed story. He took two or three spoonfuls in rapid succession of his half-melted ice-cream. Even though the rain and the storm had come and gone, the air was not appreciably cooler, or rather it was no less heavy and stagnant. Our waitress had apparently given us up as lost souls, and I glanced a little deprecatingly at the notice, 'No gratuities', on the wall.

'How long did the drought last after that?' I inquired at last.

'The drought?' said my friend. 'The questions you ask! Why, it broke that very night. Over an inch of rain we had in less than eight hours.'

'Well, that, at any rate, I suppose, was something of a comfort.'

'I don't see quite why,' he retorted.

'And then you informed the police?'

'On the Sunday.' He took out a coloured silk handkerchief from the pocket of his neat pepper-and-salt jacket, and blew his nose. It is strange how one can actually anticipate merely from the general look of a man such minute particulars as the trumpeting of a nose. Strange, I mean, that all the parts and

37

properties of human beings seem to hang so closely together, as if in positive collusion. Anyhow, the noise resounded through the glass-walled marbled room as sharp as a cockcrow.

'Well,' he said, 'that's where I stand. Looking at me, you wouldn't suppose perhaps that everything that a man wants most in this world has been destroyed and poisoned away. I had no call perhaps to be confiding in a mere stranger. But you couldn't credit the relief. I have nothing left now. I came up here to lose myself in the noise – so shocking quiet it is, there, now. But I have to go back – can't sleep much, though: wake up shouting. But what's worst is the emptiness: it's all perished. I don't want anything now. I'd as lief die and have done with it, if I could do it undriven. I've never seen a desert, but I reckon I know what the inside of one's like now. I stop thinking sometimes, and get dressed without knowing it. You wouldn't guess that from my appearance, I dare say. But once begin living as you feel underneath living *is*, where would most of us be? They have hounded me on and they've hounded me down, and presently they'll be sealing me up, and me never knowing from one day to another what news may come of – of our friend. And my sister gone and all.'

'She isn't "missing" too, I hope?' As I reflect on it, it was a vile question to have put to the man. I don't see how anything could have justified it. His face was like a burnt-out boat. The effect on him was atrocious to witness. His swarthy cheek went grey as ashes. The hand on the marble table began to tremble violently.

'Missing?' he cried. 'She's *dead*. Isn't *that* good enough for you?'

At this, no doubt because I was hopelessly in the wrong, I all but lost control of myself.

'What do you mean?' I exclaimed in a low voice. 'What do you mean by speaking to me like that? Haven't I wasted the better part of a Saturday afternoon listening to a story which, if I cared, I could read in your own county newspaper? What's it all to me, may I ask? I want to have nothing more to do with it – or you either.'

'You didn't say that at the beginning,' he replied furiously, struggling to his feet. 'You led me on.'

'Let you on, by God! What do you mean by such a piece of impudence? I say I want nothing more to do with you. And if that's how you accept a kindness, take my advice and keep your troubles to yourself in future. Let your bygones be bygones. And may the Lord have mercy on your soul.'

It was a foul outburst, due in part, I hope, to the heat; in part to the suffocating dehumanizing fetor which spreads over London when the sun has been pouring down on its bricks and mortar as fiercely as on the bones and sands of some Eastern mud village.

My stranger had sat down again abruptly, had pushed his ice away from him and covered his face with his hands. His shoulders were jumping as if with hiccups. It was fortunate perhaps that at the moment there was no other eater in the café. But the waitresses were clustered together at the counter. They must have been watching us for some little time. And the manageress was there, too, looking at us like a scandalized hen over her collar through her pince-nez. We were evidently causing a disturbance – on the brink of a 'scene'. A visionary placard flaunted across my inward eye: *Fracas in a Restaurant*.

I too sat down, and beckoned peremptorily to the young lady who had been so attentive about the bus.

'My bill, please,' I said – 'this gentleman's and mine.' And then, foolishly, I added, 'It's hot, isn't it?'

She made no reply until, after damping her lead pencil, she had added up her figures and had handed me between her finger-tips the mean scrap of paper. Then she informed me crisply, in fastidious Cockney, that some people seemed to find it hotter than most, and that it was past closing time, and would I please pay at the desk.

My accomplice had regained a little of his self-restraint by now. He put out a wavering hand and took up his hard felt hat. It was almost incredible that so marked a change should have come over so insensitive a face in that brief space of time. Its touch of bravado, its cold clear stare as of a watchful dog, even the neatness of it, had disappeared. He looked ten years older – lost and abandoned. He put out his other hand for the check. It was a curious action for a man with an intense closeness – if not meanness – clearly visible on his features. 'I should prefer, if you don't mind, to pay my bill myself,' he said.

'Not at all,' I replied brusquely. 'It was my ice-cream. I must apologize for having been so abrupt.'

He tried to smile; and it was like the gleam of a sickly evening sunshine after heavy winter rain.

'It's broken me: that's all I can say,' he said. 'What I say is you read such things in the newspapers, but you don't know what they mean to them as are most concerned. I don't see how you can. But anyhow, I can pay my way.'

I hesitated. A furious contest – dim spread-eagled figures silhouetted, as it were, against a background of utter black – seemed to be proceeding in some dream in my mind, a little beyond actual consciousness. 'Well,' I blurted, 'I hope time will make things better. I can guess what I should feel like myself in similar circumstances. If I were you, I should… ' But at sight of him, the words, I am thankful to say, faded out before I could utter them. 'If I were you' – how easy! But how is that metamorphosis conceivable?

He looked at his hat; he looked at his ice-cream, now an insipid mush; he looked anxiously and searchingly at the table – marked over with the hieroglyphics of dark ugly marble. And at last he raised his eyes – those inexpressive balls of glass – and looked at me. He changed his hat from his right to his left hand, and still looking at me, hesitated, holding the empty hand out a little above the table. Then turning away, he drew it back.

I pretended not to have noticed the action. 'There should be another Eighteen in a few minutes,' I volunteered. 'And I think I noticed a stopping-place a few yards down.'

Nevertheless I couldn't for the moment leave him there – to the tender mercies of those censorious young waitresses in their exquisitely starched caps. 'I am going that way,' I said. 'Shall I see you into it?'

'It's the heat,' he said. 'No, thank you. You have been a… '

With a gasp I repelled as well as I could the distaste for him that was once more curdling as if with a few drops of vinegar my very blood. What monsters of hatred and uncharitableness we humans can be! And what will *my* little record look like, I wonder, when the secrets of all hearts are opened.

It seemed for the time being as though the whole of my right arm had become partially paralysed. But with an effort I put out my hand at last; and then he, too, his – a large green solitaire cuff-link showing itself against his wristband as he did so. We shook hands – though I doubt if a mere fleshly contact can express much while the self behind it is dumb with instinctive distaste.

Besides, the effect on him even of a friendly action as frigid as this was horribly disconcerting. It reminded me of ice pitted and crumbling in a sudden thaw. He seemed to have been reduced to a state of physical and spiritual helplessness as if by an extremity of emotion, or by a drug. It was nauseating. It confused me and made me ashamed and miserable. I turned away abruptly; paid our bill at the desk, and went out. And London enveloped me.

The Almond Tree

My old friend, 'the Count' as we used to call him, made very strange acquaintances at times. Let but a man have plausibility, a point of view, a crotchet, an enthusiasm, he would find in him an eager and exhilarating listener. And though he was often deceived and disappointed in his finds, the Count had a heart proof against lasting disillusionment. I confess, however, that these planetary cronies of his were rather disconcerting at times. And I own that meeting him one afternoon in the busy High Street, with a companion on his arm even more than usually voluble and odd – I own I crossed the road to avoid meeting the pair.

But the Count's eyes had been too sharp for me. He twitted me unmercifully with my snobbishness. 'I am afraid we must have appeared to avoid you to-day,' he said; and received my protestations with contemptuous indifference.

But the next afternoon we took a walk together over the heath; and perhaps the sunshine, something in the first freshness of the May weather, reminded him of bygone days.

'You remember that rather out-of-the-world friend of mine yesterday that so shocked your spruce proprieties, Richard? Well, I'll tell you a story.'

As closely as I can recall this story of the Count's childhood I have related it. I wish, though, I had my old friend's gift for such things; then, perhaps, his story might retain something of the charm in the reading which he gave to it in the telling. Perhaps that charm lies wholly in the memory of his voice, his companionship, his friendship. To revive these, what task would be a burden?...

'The house of my first remembrance, the house that to my last hour on earth will seem home to me, stood in a small green hollow on the verge of a wide heath. Its five upper windows faced far eastwards towards the weather-cocked tower of a village which rambled down the steep inclination of a hill. And, walking in its green old garden – ah, Richard, the crocuses, the wallflowers, the violets! – you could see in the evening the standing fields of corn, and the dark furrows where the evening star was stationed; and a little to the south, upon a crest, a rambling wood of fir-trees and bracken.

'The house, the garden, the deep quiet orchard, all had been a wedding gift to my mother from a great-aunt, a very old lady in a kind of turban, whose shrewd eyes used to watch me out of her picture sitting in my high cane chair at meal-times – with not a little keenness; sometimes, I fancied, with a faint derision. Here passed by, to the singing of the lark, and the lamentation of autumn wind and rain, the first long nine of all these heaped-up inextricable years. Even now, my heart leaps up with longing to see again with those untutored eyes the lofty clouds of evening; to hear again as then I heard it the two small notes of the yellow-hammer piping from his green spray. I remember every room of the old house, the steep stairs, the cool apple-scented pantry; I remember the cobbles by the scullery, the well, my old dead raven, the bleak and whistling elms; but best of all I remember the unmeasured splendour of the heath, with its gorse, and its deep canopy of sunny air, the haven of every wild bird of the morning.

'Martha Rodd was a mere prim snippet of a maid then, pale and grave, with large contemplative, Puritan eyes. Mrs Ryder, in her stiff blue martial print and twisted gold brooch, was cook. And besides these, there was only old Thomas the gardener (as out-of-doors, and as distantly seen a creature as a dryad); my mother; and that busy-minded little boy, agog in wits and stomach and spirit – myself. For my father seemed but a familiar guest in the house, a guest ever eagerly desired and welcome, but none too eager to remain. He was a dark man with grey eyes and a long chin; a face unusually impassive, unusually mobile. Just as his capricious mood suggested, our little household was dejected or wildly gay. I never shall forget the spirit of delight he could conjure up at a whim, when my mother would go singing up and down stairs, and in her tiny parlour; and Martha in perfect content would prattle endlessly on to the cook, basting the twirling sirloin, while I watched in the firelight. And the long summer evenings too, when my father would find a secret, a magic, a mystery in everything; and we would sit together in the orchard while he told me tales, with the small green apples overhead, and beyond contorted branches, the first golden twilight of the moon.

'It's an old picture now, Richard, but true to the time.

'My father's will, his word, his caprice, his frown, these were the tables of the law in that small household. To my mother he was the very meaning of her life. Only that little boy was in some wise independent, busy, inquisitive, docile, sedate; though urged to a bitterness of secret rebellion at times. In his childhood he experienced such hours of distress as the years do not in mercy bring again to a heart that may analyse as well as remember. Yet there also sank to rest the fountain of life's happiness. In among the gorse bushes were the green mansions of the fairies; along the furrows before his adventurous eyes stumbled crooked gnomes, hopped bewitched robins. Ariel trebled in the sunbeams and glanced from the dewdrops; and he heard the echo of distant and magic waters in the falling of the rain.

'But my father was never long at peace in the house. Nothing satisfied him; he must needs be at an extreme. And if he was compelled to conceal his discontent, there was something so bitter and imperious in his silence, so scornful a sarcasm in his speech, that we could scarcely bear it. And the knowledge of the influence he had over us served only at such times to sharpen his contempt.

'I remember one summer's evening we had been gathering strawberries. I carried a little wicker basket, and went rummaging under the aromatic leaves, calling ever and again my mother to see the "tremenjous" berry I had found. Martha was busy beside me, vexed that her two hands could not serve her master quick enough. And in a wild race with my mother my father helped us pick. At every ripest one he took her in his arms to force it between her lips; and of those pecked by the birds he made a rhymed offering to Pan. And when the sun had descended behind the hill, and the clamour of the rooks had begun to wane in the elm-tops, he took my mother on his arm, and we trooped all together up the long straggling path, and across the grass, carrying our spoil of fruit into the cool dusky corridor. As we passed into the gloaming I saw my mother stoop impulsively and kiss his arm. He brushed off her hand impatiently, and went into his study. I heard the door shut. A moment afterwards he called for candles. And, looking on those two other faces in the twilight, I knew with the intuition of childhood that he was suddenly sick to death of us all; and I knew that my mother shared my intuition. She sat down, and I beside her, in her little parlour, and took up her sewing. But her face had lost again all its girlishness as she bent her head over the white linen.

'I think she was happier when my father was away; for then, free from anxiety to be for ever pleasing his variable moods, she could entertain herself with hopes and preparations for his return. There was a little summer-house, or arbour, in the garden, where she would sit alone, while the swallows coursed in the evening air. Sometimes, too, she would take me for a long walk, listening distantly to my chatter, only, I think, that she might entertain the pleasure of supposing that my father might have returned home unforeseen, and be even now waiting to greet us. But these fancies would forsake her. She would speak harshly and coldly to me, and scold Martha for her owlishness, and find nothing but vanity and mockery in all that but a little while since had been her daydream.

'I think she rarely knew where my father stayed in his long absences from home. He would remain with us for a week, and neglect us for a month. She was too proud, and when he was himself, too happy and hopeful to question him, and he seemed to delight in keeping his affairs secret from her. Indeed, he sometimes appeared to pretend a mystery where none was, and to endeavour in all things to make his character and conduct appear quixotic and inexplicable.

'So time went on. Yet, it seemed, as each month passed by, the house was not so merry and happy as before; something was fading and vanishing that would not return; estrangement had pierced a little deeper. I think care at last put out of my mother's mind even the semblance of her former gaiety. She sealed up her heart lest love should break forth anew into the bleakness.

'On Guy Fawkes' Day Martha told me at bedtime that a new household had moved into the village on the other side of the heath. After that my father stayed away from us but seldom.

'At first my mother showed her pleasure in a thousand ways, with dainties of her own fancy and cooking, with ribbons in her dark hair, with new songs (though she had but a small thin voice). She read to please him; and tired my legs out in useless errands in his service. And a word of praise sufficed her for many hours of difficulty. But by and by, when evening after evening was spent by my father away from home, she began to be uneasy and depressed; and though she made no complaint, her anxious face, the incessant interrogation of her eyes vexed and irritated him beyond measure.

'"Where does my father go after dinner?" I asked Martha one night, when my mother was in my bedroom, folding my clothes.

'"How dare you ask such a question?" said my mother, "and how dare you talk to the child about your master's comings and goings?"

'"But where does he?" I repeated to Martha, when my mother was gone out of the room.

'"Ssh now, Master Nicholas," she answered, "didn't you hear what your mamma said? She's vexed, poor lady, at master's never spending a whole day at home, but nothing but them cards, cards, cards, every night at Mr Grey's. Why, often it's twelve and one in the morning when I've heard his foot on the gravel beneath the window. But there, I'll be bound, she doesn't *mean* to speak unkindly. It's a terrible scourge is jealousy, Master Nicholas; and not generous or manly to give it cause. Mrs Ryder was kept a widow all along of jealousy, and but a week before her wedding with her second."

'"But why is mother jealous of my father playing cards?"

'Martha slipped my nightgown over my head. "Ssh, Master Nicholas, little boys mustn't ask so many questions. And I hope when you are grown up to be a man, my dear, you will be a comfort to your mother. She needs it, poor soul, and sakes alive, just now of all times!" I looked inquisitively into Martha's face; but she screened my eyes with her hand; and instead of further questions, I said my prayers to her.

'A few days after this I was sitting with my mother in her parlour, holding her grey worsted for her to wind, when my father entered the room and bade me put on my hat and muffler. "He is going to pay a call with me," he explained curtly. As I went out of the room, I heard my mother's question, "To your friends at the Grange, I suppose?"

'"You may suppose whatever you please," he answered. I heard my mother rise to leave the room, but he called her back and the door was shut…

'The room in which the card-players sat was very low-ceiled. A piano stood near the window, a rosewood table with a fine dark crimson work-basket upon it by the fireside, and some little distance away, a green card-table with candles burning.

Mr Grey was a slim, elegant man, with a high, narrow forehead and long fingers. Major Aubrey was a short, red-faced, rather taciturn man. There was also a younger man with fair hair. They seemed to be on the best of terms together; and I helped to pack the cards and to pile the silver coins, sipping a glass of sherry with Mr Grey. My father said little, paying me no attention, but playing gravely with a very slight frown.

'After some little while the door opened, and a lady appeared. This was Mr Grey's sister, Jane, I learned. She seated herself at her work-table, and drew me to her side.

'"Well, so this is Nicholas!" she said. "Or is it Nick?"

'"Nicholas," I said.

'"Of course," she said, smiling, "and I like that too, much the best. How very kind of you to come to see me! It was to keep *me* company, you know, because I am very stupid at games, but I love talking. Do you?"

'I looked into her eyes, and knew we were friends. She smiled again, with open lips, and touched my mouth with her thimble. "Now, let me see, business first, and – me afterwards. You see I have three different kinds of cake, because, I thought, I cannot in the least tell which kind he'll like best. Could I now? Come, you shall choose."

'She rose and opened the long door of a narrow cupboard, looking towards the card-players as she stooped. I remember the cakes to this day; little oval shortbreads stamped with a beehive, custards and mince-pies; and a great glass jar of goodies which I carried in both arms round the little square table. I took a mince-pie, and sat down on a footstool near by Miss Grey, and she talked to me while she worked with slender hands at her lace embroidery. I told her how old I was; about my great-aunt and her three cats. I told her my dreams, and that I was very fond of Yorkshire pudding, "from under the meat, you know". And I told her I thought my father the handsomest man I had ever seen.

'"What, handsomer than Mr Spencer?" she said laughing, looking along her needle.

'I answered that I did not very much like clergymen.

'"And why?" she said gravely.

'"Because they do not talk like real," I said.

'She laughed very gaily. "Do men ever?" she said.

'And her voice was so quiet and so musical, her neck so graceful, I thought her a very beautiful lady, admiring especially her dark eyes when she smiled brightly and yet half sadly at me; I promised, moreover, that if she would meet me on the heath, I would show her the rabbit warren and the "Miller's Pool".

'"Well, Jane, and what do you think of my son?" said my father when we were about to leave.

'She bent over me and squeezed a lucky fourpenny-piece into my hand. "I love fourpence, pretty little fourpence, I love fourpence better than my life," she whispered into my ear. "But that's a secret," she added, glancing up over her shoulder. She kissed lightly the top of my head. I was looking at my father while she was caressing me, and I fancied a faint sneer passed over his face. But when we had come out of the village on to the heath, in the bare keen night, as we walked along the path together between the gorse-bushes, now on turf, and now on stony ground, never before had he seemed so wonderful a companion. He told me little stories; he began a hundred, and finished none; yet with the stars above us, they seemed a string of beads all of bright colours. We stood still in the vast darkness, while he whistled that strangest of all old songs – "the Song the Sirens sang". He pilfered my wits and talked like my double. But when – how much too quickly, I thought with sinking heart – we were come to the house-gates, he suddenly fell silent, turned an instant, and stared far away over the windy heath.

'"How weary, flat, stale – " he began, and broke off between uneasy laughter and a sigh. "Listen to me, Nicholas," he said, lifting my face to the starlight, "you must grow up a man – a Man, you understand; no vapourings, no posings, no caprices; and above all, no sham. No sham. It's your one and only chance in this unfaltering Scheme." He scanned my face long and closely. "You have your mother's eyes," he said musingly. "And that," he added under his breath, "*that's* no joke." He pushed open the squealing gate and we went in.

'My mother was sitting in a low chair before a dying and cheerless fire.

'"Well, Nick," she said very suavely, "and how have you enjoyed your evening?"

'I stared at her without answer. "Did you play cards with the gentlemen; or did you turn over the music?"

'"I talked to Miss Grey," I said.

'"Really," said my mother, raising her eyebrows, "and who then is Miss Grey?" My father was smiling at us with sparkling eyes.

'"Mr Grey's sister," I answered in a low voice.

'"Not his wife, then?" said my mother, glancing furtively at the fire. I looked towards my father in doubt but could lift my eyes no higher than his knees.

'"You little fool!" he said to my mother with a laugh, "what a sharpshooter! Never mind, Sir Nick; there, run off to bed, my man."

'My mother caught me roughly by the sleeve as I was passing her chair. "Aren't you going to kiss me good night, then," she said furiously, her narrow under-lip quivering, "you too!" I kissed her cheek. "That's right, my dear," she said scornfully, "that's how little fishes kiss." She rose and drew back her skirts. "I refuse to stay in the room," she said haughtily and with a sob she hurried out.

'My father continued to smile, but only a smile it seemed gravity had forgotten to smooth away. He stood very still, so still that I grew afraid he must certainly hear me thinking. Then with a kind of sigh he sat down at my mother's writing table, and scribbled a few words with his pencil on a slip of paper.

'"There, Nicholas, just tap at your mother's door with that. Good night, old fellow," he took my hand and smiled down into my eyes with a kind of generous dark appeal that called me straight to his side. I hastened conceitedly upstairs, and delivered my message. My mother was crying when she opened the door.

'"Well?" she said in a low, trembling voice.

'But presently afterwards, while I was still lingering in the dark corridor, I heard her run down quickly, and in a while my father and mother came upstairs together, arm in arm, and by her light talk and laughter you might suppose she had no knowledge of care or trouble at all.

'Never afterwards did I see so much gaiety and youthfulness in my mother's face as when she sat next morning with us at breakfast. The honeycomb, the small bronze chrysanthemums, her yellow gown seemed dainty as a miniature. With every word her eyes would glance covertly at my father; her smile, as it were, hesitating between her lashes. She was so light and girlish and so versatile I should scarcely have recognized the weary and sallow face of the night before. My father seemed to find as much pleasure, or relief, in her good spirits as I did; and to delight in exercising his ingenuity to quicken her humour.

'It was but a transient morning of sunshine, however, and as the brief and sombre day waned, its gloom pervaded the house. In the evening my father left us to our solitude as usual. And that night was very misty over the heath, with a small, warm rain falling.

'So it happened that I began to be left more and more to my own devices, and grew so inured at last to my own narrow company and small thoughts and cares, that I began to look on my mother's unhappiness almost with indifference, and learned to criticize almost before I had learned to pity. And so I do not think I enjoyed Christmas very much the less, although my father was away from home and all our little festivities were dispirited. I had plenty of good things to eat, and presents, and a picture-book from Martha. I had a new rocking-horse – how changeless and impassive its mottled battered face looks out at me across the years! It was brisk, clear weather, and on St Stephen's Day I went to see if there was any ice yet on the Miller's Pool.

'I was stooping down at the extreme edge of the pool, snapping the brittle splinters of the ice with my finger, when I heard a voice calling me in the still air. It was Jane Grey, walking on the heath with my father, who had called me having seen me from a distance stooping beside the water.

'"So you see I have kept my promise," she said, taking my hand.

'"But you promised to come by yourself," I said.

'"Well, so I will then," she answered, nodding her head. "Good-bye," she added, turning to my father. "It's three's none, you see. Nicholas shall take me home to tea, and you can call for him in the evening, if you will; that is, if you are coming."

'"Are you asking me to come?" he said moodily, "do you care whether I come or not?"

'She lifted her face and spoke gravely. "You are my friend," she said, "of course I care whether you are with me or not." He scrutinized her through half-closed lids. His face was haggard, gloomy with *ennui*. "How you harp on the word, you punctilious Jane. Do you suppose I am still in my teens? Twenty years ago, now – It amuses me to hear you women talk. It's little you ever really feel."

'"I don't think I am quite without feeling," she replied, "you are a little difficult, you know."

'"Difficult," he echoed in derision. He checked himself and shrugged his shoulders. "You see, Jane, it's all on the surface; I boast of my indifference. It's the one rag of philosophy age denies no one. It is so easy to be mock-heroic – debonair, iron-grey, rhetorical, dramatic – you know it only too well, perhaps? But after all, life's comedy, when one stops smiling, is only the tepidest farce. Or the gilt wears off and the pinchbeck tragedy shows through. And so, as I say, we talk on, being past feeling. One by one our hopes come home to roost, our delusions find themselves out, and the mystery proves to be nothing but sleight-of-hand. It's age, my dear Jane – age; it turns one to stone. With you young people life's a dream; ask Nicholas here!" He shrugged his shoulders, adding under his breath, "But one wakes on a devilish hard pallet."

'"Of course," said Jane slowly, "you are only talking cleverly, and then it does not matter whether it's true or not, I suppose. I can't say. I don't think you mean it, and so it comes to nothing. I can't and won't believe you feel so little – I can't." She continued to smile, yet, I fancied, with the brightness of tears in her eyes. "It's all mockery and make-believe; we are not the miserable slaves of time you try to fancy. There must be some way to win through." She turned away, then added slowly, "You ask me to be fearless, sincere, to speak my heart; I wonder, do you?"

'My father did not look at her, appeared not to have seen the hand she had half held out to him and as swiftly withdrawn. "The truth is, Jane," he said slowly, "I am past sincerity now. And as for *heart* it is a quite discredited organ at forty. Life, thought, selfishness, egotism, call it what you will; they have all done their worst with me; and I really haven't the sentiment to pretend that they haven't. And when bright youth and senti-ment are gone; why, go too, dear lady! Existence proves nothing but brazen inanity afterwards. But there's always that turning left to the dullest and dustiest road – oblivion." He remained silent a moment. Silence deep and strange lay all around us. The air was still, the wintry sky unutterably calm. And again that low dispassionate voice continued: "It's only when right seems too easy a thing, too trivial, and not worth the doing; and wrong a foolish thing – too dull… There, take care of her, Nicholas; take care of her, 'snips and snails,' you know. *Au revoir*, 'pon my word, I almost wish it was good-bye."

'Jane Grey regarded him attentively. "So then do I," she replied in a low voice, "for I shall never understand you; perhaps I should hate to understand you."

'My father turned with an affected laugh, and left us.

'Miss Grey and I walked slowly along beside the frosty bulrushes until we came to the wood. The bracken and heather were faded. The earth was dark and rich with autumnal rains. Fir-cones lay on the moss beneath the dark green branches. It was all now utterly silent in the wintry afternoon. Far away rose tardily, and alighted, the hoarse rooks upon the ploughed earth; high in the pale sky passed a few on ragged wing.

'"What does my father mean by wishing it was good-bye?" I said.

'But my companion did not answer me in words. She clasped my hand; she seemed very slim and gracious walking by my side on the hardened ground. My mother was small now and awkward beside her in my imagination. I questioned her about the ice, about the red sky, and if there was any mistletoe in the woods. Sometimes she, in turn, asked me questions too, and when I answered them we would look at each other and smile, and it seemed it was with her as it was with me – of the pure gladness I found in her company. In the middle of our walk to the Thorns she bent down in the cold twilight, and putting her hands on my shoulders, "My dear, dear Nicholas," she said, "you must be a good son to your mother – brave and kind; will you?"

'"He hardly ever speaks to mother now," I answered instinctively.

'She pressed her lips to my cheek, and her cheek was cold against mine, and she clasped her arms about me. "Kiss me," she said, "We must do our best, mustn't we?" she pleaded, still holding me. I looked mournfully into the gathering darkness. "That's easy when you're grown up," I said. She laughed and kissed me again, and then we took hands and ran till we were out of breath, towards the distant lights of the Thorns...

'I had been some time in bed, lying awake in the warmth, when my mother came softly through the darkness into my room. She sat down at the bedside, breathing hurriedly. "Where have you been all the evening?" she said.

'"Miss Grey asked me to stay to tea," I answered.

'"Did I give you permission to go to tea with Miss Grey?"

'I made no answer.

'"If you go to that house again, I shall beat you. You hear me, Nicholas? Alone, or with your father, if you go there again, without my permission, I shall beat you. You have not been whipped for a long time, have you?" I could not see her face, but her head was bent towards me in the dark, as she sat – almost crouched – on my bedside.

'I made no answer. But when my mother had gone, without kissing me, I cried noiselessly on in to my pillow. Something had suddenly flown out of memory, never to sing again. Life had become a little colder and stranger. I had always been my own chief company; now another sentimental barrier had arisen between the world and me, past its heedlessness, past my understanding to break down.

'Hardly a week passed now without some bitter quarrel. I seemed to be perpetually stealing out of sound of angry voices; fearful of being made the butt of my father's serene taunts, of my mother's passions and desperate remorse. He disdained to defend himself against her, never reasoned with her; he merely shrugged his shoulders, denied her charges, ignored her anger; coldly endeavouring only to show his indifference, to conceal by every means in his power his own inward weariness and vexation. I saw this, of course, only vaguely, yet with all a child's certainty of insight, though I rarely knew the cause of my misery; and I continued to love them both in my selfish fashion, not a whit the less.

'At last, on St Valentine's Day, things came to a worse pass than ever. It had always been my father's custom to hang my mother a valentine on the handle of her little parlour door, a string of pearls, a fan, a book of poetry, whatever it might be. She came down early this morning, and sat in the window-seat, looking out at the falling snow. She said nothing at breakfast, only feigned to eat, lifting her eyes at intervals to glance at my father with a strange intensity, as if of hatred, tapping her foot on the floor. He took no notice of her, sat quiet and moody with his own thoughts. I think he had not really forgotten the day, for I found long afterwards in his old bureau a bracelet purchased but a week before with her name written on a scrap of paper, inside the case. Yet it seemed to be the absence of this little gift that had driven my mother beyond reason.

'Towards evening, tired of the house, tired of being alone, I went out and played for a while listlessly in the snow. At night-fall I went in; and in the dark heard angry voices. My father came out of the dining-room and looked at me in silence, standing in the gloom of the wintry dusk. My mother followed him. I can see her now, leaning in the doorway, white with rage, her eyes ringed and darkened with continuous trouble, her hand trembling.

'"It shall learn to hate you," she cried in a low, dull voice. "I will teach it every moment to hate and despise you as I – Oh, *I* hate and despise you."

59

'My father looked at her calmly and profoundly before replying. He took up a cloth hat and brushed it with his hand. "Very well then, you have chosen," he said coldly. "It has always lain with you. You have exaggerated, you have raved, and now you have said what can never be recalled or forgotten. Here's Nicholas. Pray do not imagine, however, that I am defending myself. I have nothing to defend. I think of no one but myself – no one. Endeavour to understand me, no one. Perhaps, indeed, you yourself – no more than – But words again – the dull old round!" He made a peculiar gesture with his hand. "Well, life is... ach! I have done. So be it." He stood looking out of the door. "You see, it's snowing," he said, as if to himself.

'All the long night before and all day long, snow had been falling continuously. The air was wintry and cold. I could discern nothing beyond the porch but a gloomy accumulation of cloud in the twilight air, now darkened with the labyrinthine motion of the snow. My father glanced back for an instant into the house, and, as I fancy, regarded me with a kind of strange, close earnestness. But he went out and his footsteps were instantly silenced.

'My mother peered at me in a dreadful perplexity, her eyes wide with terror and remorse. "What? What?" she said. I stared at her stupidly. Three snowflakes swiftly and airily floated together into the dim hall from the gloom without. She clasped her hand over her mouth. Overburdened her fingers seemed to be, so slender were they, with her many rings.

'"Nicholas, Nicholas, tell me; what was I saying? What was I saying?" She stumbled hastily to the door. "Arthur, Arthur," she cried from the porch, "it's St Valentine's Day. That was all I meant; come back, come back!" But perhaps my father was already out of hearing; I do not think he made any reply.

'My mother came in doubtfully, resting her hand on the wall. And she walked very slowly and laboriously upstairs. While I was standing at the foot of the staircase, looking out across the hall into the evening, Martha climbed primly up from the kitchen with her lighted taper, shut-to the door and lit the hall lamp. Already the good smell of the feast cooking floated up from the kitchen, and gladdened my spirits. "Will he come back?" Martha said, looking very scared in the light of her taper. "It's such a fall of snow, already it's a hand's breadth on the window-sill. Oh, Master Nicholas, it's a hard world for us women." She followed my mother upstairs, carrying light to all the gloomy upper rooms.

'I sat down in the window-seat of the dining-room, and read in my picture-book as well as I could by the flame-light. By and by, Martha returned to lay the table.

'As far back as brief memory carried me, it had been our custom to make a Valentine's feast on the Saint's day. This was my father's mother's birthday also. When she was alive I well remember her visiting us with her companion, Miss Schreiner, who talked in such good-humoured English to me. This same anniversary had last year brought about a tender reconciliation between my father and mother, after a quarrel that meant how little then. And I remember on this day to have seen the first fast-sealed buds upon the almond tree. We would have a great spangled cake in the middle of the table, with marzipan and comfits, just as at Christmas-time. And when Mrs Merry lived in the village, her little fair daughters used to come in a big carriage to spend the evening with us and to share my Valentine's feast.

'But all this was changed now. My wits were sharper, but I was none the less only the duller for that; my hopes and dreams had a little fallen and faded. I looked idly at my picture-book, vaguely conscious that its colours pleased me less than once upon a time; that I was rather tired of seeing them, and they just as tired of seeing me. And yet I had nothing else to do, so I must go on with a hard face, turning listlessly the pictured pages.

'About seven o'clock my mother sent for me. I found her sitting in her bedroom. Candles were burning before the looking-glass. She was already dressed in her handsome black silk gown, and wearing her pearl necklace. She began to brush my hair, curling its longer ends with her fingers, which she moistened in the pink bowl that was one of the first things I had set eyes on in this world. She put me on a clean blouse and my buckle shoes, talking to me the while, almost as if she were telling me a story. Then she looked at herself long and earnestly in the glass; throwing up her chin with a smile, as was a habit of hers in talk. I wandered about the room, fingering the little toilet-boxes and nick-nacks on the table. By mischance I upset one of these, a scent-bottle that held rose-water. The water ran out and filled the warm air with its fragrance. "You foolish, clumsy boy!" said my mother, and slapped my hand. More out of vexation and tiredness than because of the pain, I began to cry. And then, with infinite tenderness, she leaned her head on my shoulder. "Mother can't think very well just now," she said; and cried so bitterly in silence that I was only too ready to extricate myself and run away when her hold on me relaxed.

'I climbed slowly upstairs to Martha's bedroom, and kneeling on a cane chair looked out of the window. The flakes had ceased to fall now, although the snowy heath was encompassed in mist. Above the snow the clouds had parted, drifting from beneath the stars, and these in their constellations were trembling very brightly, and here and there burned one of them in solitude, larger and wilder in its radiance than the rest. But though I did not tire of looking out of the window, my knees began to ache; and the little room was very cold and still so near the roof. So I went down to the dining-room, with all its seven candlesticks kindled, seeming to my unaccustomed eyes a very splendid blaze out of the dark. My mother was kneeling on the rug by the fireside. She looked very small, even dwarfish, I thought. She was gazing into the flames; one shoe curved beneath the hem of her gown, her chin resting on her hand.

'I surveyed the table with its jellies and sweetmeats and glasses and fruit, and began to be very hungry, so savoury was the smell of the turkey roasting downstairs. Martha knocked at the door when the clock had struck eight.

'"Dinner is ready, ma'am."

'My mother glanced fleetingly at the clock. "Just a little, only a very little while longer, tell Mrs Ryder; your master will be home in a minute." She rose and placed the claret in the hearth at some distance from the fire.

'"Is it nicer warm, Mother?" I said. She looked at me with startled eyes and nodded. "Did you hear anything, Nicholas? Run to the door and listen; was that a sound of footsteps?"

'I opened the outer door and peered into the darkness; but it seemed the world ended here with the warmth and the light: beyond could extend only winter and silence, a region that, familiar though it was to me, seemed now to terrify me like an enormous sea.

'"It's stopped snowing," I said, "but there isn't anybody there; nobody at all, Mother."

'The hours passed heavily from quarter on to quarter. The turkey, I grieved to hear, was to be taken out of the oven, and put away to cool in the pantry. I was bidden help myself to what I pleased of the trembling jellies, and delicious pink blanc-mange. Already midnight would be the next hour to be chimed. I felt sick, yet was still hungry and very tired. The candles began to burn low. "Leave me a little light here, then," my mother said at last to Martha, "and go to bed. Perhaps your master has missed his way home in the snow." But Mrs Ryder had followed Martha into the room.

'"You must pardon my interference, ma'am, but it isn't right, it isn't really right of you to sit up longer. Master will not come back, maybe, before morning. And I shouldn't be doing my bounden duty, ma'am, except I spoke my mind. Just now too, of all times."

'"Thank you very much, Mrs Ryder," my mother answered simply "but I would prefer not to go to bed yet. It's very lonely on the heath at night. But I shall not want anything else, thank you."

'"Well, ma'am, I've had my say, and done my conscience's bidding. And I have brought you up this tumbler of mulled wine; else you'll be sinking away or something with the fatigue."

'My mother took the wine, sipped of it with a wan smile at Mrs Ryder over the brim; and Mrs Ryder retired with Martha. I don't think they had noticed me sitting close in the shadow on my stool beside the table. But all through that long night, I fancy, these good souls took it in turn to creep down stealthily and look in on us; and in the small hours of the morning, when the fire had fallen low they must have wrapped us both warm in shawls. They left me then, I think, to be my mother's company. Indeed, I remember we spoke in the darkness, and she took my hand.

'My mother and I shared the steaming wine together when they were gone; our shadows looming faintly huge upon the ceiling. We said very little, but I looked softly into her grey childish eyes, and we kissed one another kneeling there to-gether before the fire. And afterwards, I jigged softly round the table, pilfering whatever sweet or savoury mouthful took my fancy. But by and by in the silent house – a silence broken only by the fluttering of the flames, and the odd far-away stir of the frost, drowsiness vanquished me; I sat down by the fireside, leaning my head on a chair. And sitting thus, vaguely eyeing firelight and wavering shadow, I began to nod, and very soon dream stalked in, mingling with reality.

'It was early morning when I awoke, dazed and cold and miserable in my uncomfortable resting-place. The rare odour of frost was on the air. The ashes of the fire lay iron-grey upon the cold hearth. An intensely clear white ray of light leaned up through a cranny of the shutters to the cornice of the ceiling. I got up with difficulty. My mother was still asleep, breathing heavily, and as I stooped, regarding her curiously, I could almost watch her transient dreams fleeting over her face; and now she smiled faintly; and now she raised her eyebrows as if in some playful and happy talk with my father; then again utterly still darkness would descend on brow and lid and lip.

'I touched her sleeve, suddenly conscious of my loneliness in the large house. Her face clouded instantly, she sighed profoundly: "What?" she said, "nothing – nothing?" She stretched out her hand towards me; the lids drew back from eyes still blind from sleep. But gradually time regained its influence over her. She moistened her lips and turned to me, and suddenly, in a gush of agony, remembrance of the night returned to her. She hid her face in her hands, rocking her body gently to and fro; then rose and smoothed back her hair at the looking-glass. I was surprised to see no trace of tears on her cheeks. Her lips moved, as if unconsciously a heart worn out with grief addressed that pale reflection of her sorrow in the glass. I took hold of the hand that hung down listlessly on her silk skirt, and fondled it, kissing punctiliously each loose ring in turn.

'But I do not think she heeded my kisses. So I returned to the table on which was still set out the mockery of our Valentine feast, strangely disenchanted in the chill dusk of daybreak. I put a handful of wine biscuits and a broken piece of cake in my pocket; for a determination had taken me to go out on to the heath. My heart beat thick and fast in imagination of the solitary snow and of myself wandering in loneliness across its untrampled surface. A project also was forming in my mind of walking over to the Thorns; for somehow I knew my mother would not scold or punish me that day. Perhaps, I thought, my father would be there. And I would tell Miss Grey all about my adventure of the night spent down in the dining-room. So moving very stealthily, and betraying no eagerness, lest I should be forbidden to go, I stole at length unnoticed from the room, and leaving the great hall door ajar, ran out joyously into the wintry morning.

'Already dawn was clear and high in the sky, already the first breezes were moving in the mists; and breathed chill, as if it were the lingering darkness itself on my cheeks. The air was cold, yet with a fresh faint sweetness. The snow lay crisp across its perfect surface, mounded softly over the gorse-bushes, though here and there a spray of parched blossom yet pro-truded from its cowl. Flaky particles of ice floated invisible in the air. I called out with pleasure to see the little ponds where the snow had been blown away from the black ice. I saw on the bushes too the webs of spiders stretched from thorn to thorn, and festooned with crystals of hoar-frost. I turned and counted as far as I could my footsteps leading back to the house, which lay roofed in gloomy pallor, dim and obscured in the darkened west.

'A waning moon that had risen late in the night shone, it seemed, very near to the earth. But every moment light swept invincibly in, pouring its crystal like a river; and darkness sullenly withdrew into the north. And when at last the sun appeared, glittering along the rosy snow, I turned in an ecstasy and with my finger pointed him out, as if the house I had left behind me might view him with my own delight. Indeed, I saw its windows transmuted, and heard afar a thrush pealing in the bare branches of a pear-tree; and a robin startled me, so suddenly shrill and sweet he broke into song from a snowy tuft of gorse.

'I was now come to the beginning of a gradual incline, from the summit of which I should presently descry in the distance the avenue of lindens that led towards the village from the margin of the heath. As I went on my way, munching my biscuits, looking gaily about me, I brooded deliciously on the breakfast which Miss Grey would doubtless sit me down to; and almost forgot the occasion of my errand, and the troubled house I had left behind me. At length I climbed to the top of the smooth ridge and looked down. At a little distance from me grew a crimson hawthorn-tree that often in past Aprils I had used for a green tent from the showers; but now it was closely hooded, darkening with its faint shadow the long expanse of unshadowed whiteness. Not very far from this bush I perceived a figure lying stretched along the snow and knew instinctively that this was my father lying here.

'The sight did not then surprise or dismay me. It seemed only the lucid sequel to that long heavy night-watch, to all the troubles and perplexities of the past. I felt no sorrow, but stood beside the body, regarding it only with deep wonder and a kind of earnest curiosity, yet perhaps with a remote pity too, that he could not see me in the beautiful morning. His grey hand lay arched in the snow, his darkened face, on which showed a smear of dried blood, was turned away a little as if out of the oblique sunshine. I understood that he was dead, and had already begun speculating on what changes it would make; how I should spend my time; what would happen in the house now that he was gone, his influence, his authority, his discord. I remembered too that I was alone, was master of this immense secret, that I must go home sedately, as if it were a Sunday, and in a low voice tell my mother, concealing any exultation I might feel in the office. I imagined the questions that would be asked me, and was considering the proper answers to make to them, when my morbid dreams were suddenly broken in on by

Martha Rodd. She stood in my footsteps, looking down on me from the ridge from which I had but just now descended. She hastened towards me, stooping a little as if she were carrying a heavy bundle, her mouth ajar, her forehead wrinkled beneath its wispy light brown hair.

'"Look, Martha, look," I cried, "I found him in the snow; he's dead." And suddenly a bond seemed to snap in my heart. The beauty and solitude of the morning, the perfect whiteness of the snow – it was all an uncouth mockery against me – a subtle and quiet treachery. The tears gushed into my eyes and in my fear and affliction I clung to the poor girl, sobbing bitterly, protesting my grief, hiding my eyes in terror from that still, inscrutable shape. She smoothed my hair with her hand again and again, her eyes fixed; and then at last, venturing cautiously nearer, she stooped over my father. "O Master Nicholas," she said, "his poor dark hair! What will we do now? What will your poor mamma do now, and him gone?" She hid her face in her hands, and our tears gushed out anew.

'But my grief was speedily forgotten. The novelty of being left entirely alone, my own master; to go where I would; to do as I pleased; the experience of being pitied most when I least needed it, and then – when misery and solitariness came over me like a cloud – of being utterly ignored, turned my thoughts gradually away. My father's body was brought home and laid in my mother's little parlour that looked out on to the garden and the snowy orchard. The house was darkened. I took a secret pleasure in peeping in on the sunless rooms, and stealing from door to door through corridors screened from the daylight. My mother was ill; and for some inexplicable reason I connected her illness with the bevy of gentlemen dressed in black who came one morning to the house and walked away together over the heath. Finally Mrs Marshall drove up one afternoon from Islington, and by the bundles she had brought with her and her grained box with the iron handles I knew that she was come, as once before in my experience, to stay.

'I was playing on the morrow in the hall with my leaden soldiers when there came into my mind vaguely the voices of Mrs Ryder and of Mrs Marshall gossiping together on their tedious way upstairs from the kitchen.

'"No, Mrs Marshall, nothing," I heard Mrs Ryder saying, "not one word, not one word. And now the poor dear lady left quite alone, and only the doctor to gainsay that fatherless mite from facing the idle inquisitive questions of all them strangers. It's neither for me nor you, Mrs Marshall, to speak out just what comes into our heads here and now. The ways of the Almighty are past understanding – but a kinder at *heart* never trod this earth."

'"Ah," said Mrs Marshall.

'"I knew to my sorrow," continued Mrs Ryder, "there was words in the house; but there, wheresoever you be there's that. Human beings ain't angels, married or single, and in every – "

'"Wasn't there talk of some – ?" insinuated Mrs Marshall discreetly.

'"Talk, Mrs Marshall," said Mrs Ryder, coming to a standstill, "I scorn the word! A pinch of truth in a hogshead of falsehood. I don't gainsay it even. I just shut my ears – there – with the dead." Mrs Marshall had opened her mouth to reply when I was discovered, crouched as small as possible at the foot of the stairs.

'"Well, here's pitchers!" said Mrs Marshall pleasantly. "And this is the poor fatherless manikin, I suppose. It's hard on the innocent, Mrs Ryder, and him grown such a sturdy child too, as I said from the first. Well, now, and don't you remember me, little man, don't you remember Mrs Marshall? He ought to, now!"

'"He's a very good boy in general," said Mrs Ryder, "and I'm sure I hope and pray he'll grow up to be a comfort to his poor widowed mother, if so be – " They glanced earnestly at one another, and Mrs Marshall stooped with a sigh of effort and drew a big leather purse from a big loose pocket under her skirt, and selected a bright ha'penny-piece from among its silver and copper.

'"I make no doubt he will, poor mite," she said cheerfully; I took the ha'penny in silence and the two women passed slowly upstairs.

'In the afternoon, in order to be beyond call of Martha, I went out on to the heath with a shovel, intent on building a great tomb in the snow. Yet more snow had fallen during the night; it now lay so deep as to cover my socks above my shoes. I laboured very busily, shovelling, beating, moulding, stamping. So intent was I that I did not see Miss Grey until she was close beside me. I looked up from the snow and was surprised to find the sun already set and the low mists of evening approaching. Miss Grey was veiled and dressed in furs to the throat. She drew her ungloved hand from her muff.

'"Nicholas," she said in a low voice.

'I stood for some reason confused and ashamed without answering her. She sat down on my shapeless mound of snow, and took me by the hand. Then she drew up her veil, and I saw her face pale and darkened, and her clear dark eyes gravely gazing into mine.

'"My poor, poor Nicholas," she said, and continued to gaze at me with her warm hand clasping mine. "What can I say? What can I do? Isn't it very, very lonely out here in the snow?"

'"I didn't feel lonely much," I answered, "I was making a – I was playing at building."

'"And I am sitting on your beautiful snow-house, then?" she said, smiling sadly, her hand trembling upon mine.

'"It isn't a house," I answered, turning away.

'She pressed my hand on the furs at her throat.

'"Poor cold, blue hands," she said. "Do you like playing alone?"

'"I like you being here," I answered. "I wish you would come always, or at least sometimes."

'She drew me close to her, smiling, and bent and kissed my head.

'"There," she said, "I am here now."

'"Mother's ill," I said.

'She drew back and looked out over the heath towards the house.

'"They have put my father in the little parlour, in his coffin, of course; you know he's dead, and Mrs Marshall's come; she gave me a ha'penny this morning. Dr Graham gave me a whole crown, though." I took it out of my breeches pocket and showed it her.

'"That's very, very nice," she said. "What lots of nice things you can buy with it! And, look, I am going to give you a little keepsake too, between just you and me."

'It was a small silver box that she drew out of her muff, and embossed in the silver of the lid was a crucifix. "I thought, perhaps, I should see you to-day, you know," she continued softly. "Now, who's given you this?" she said, putting the box into my hand.

'"You," I answered softly.

'"And who am I?"

'"Miss Grey," I said.

'"Your friend, Jane Grey," she repeated, as if she were fascinated by the sound of her own name. "Say it now – Always my friend, Jane Grey."

'I repeated it after her.

'"And now," she continued, "tell me which room is – is the little parlour. Is it that small window at the corner under the ivy?"

'I shook my head.

'"Which?" she said in a whisper, after a long pause.

'I twisted my shovel in the snow. "Would you like to see my father?" I asked her. "I am sure, you know, Martha would not mind; and mother's in bed." She started, her dark eyes dwelling strangely on mine. "But Nicholas, you poor lamb; where?" she said, without stirring.

'"It's at the back, a little window that comes out – if you were to come this evening, I would be playing in the hall; I always play in the hall, after tea, if I can; and now, always. Nobody would see you at all, you know."

'She sighed. "O what are you saying?" she said, and stood up, drawing down her veil.

'"But would you like to?" I repeated. She stooped suddenly, pressing her veiled face to mine. "I'll come, I'll come," she said, her face utterly changed so close to my eyes. "We can both still – still be loyal to him, can't we, Nicholas?"

'She walked away quickly, towards the pool and the little darkened wood. I looked after her and knew that she would be waiting there alone till evening. I looked at my silver box with great satisfaction, and after opening it, put it into my pocket with my crown piece and my ha'penny, and continued my building for awhile.

'But now zest for it was gone; and I began to feel cold, the frost closing in keenly as darkness gathered. So I went home.

'My silence and suspicious avoidance of scrutiny and question passed unnoticed. Indeed, I ate my tea in solitude, except that now and again one or other of the women would come bustling in on some brief errand. A peculiar suppressed stir was in the house. I wondered what could be the cause of it; and began suddenly to be afraid of my project being discovered.

'None the less I was playing in the evening, as I had promised, close to the door, alert to catch the faintest sign of the coming of my visitor.

'"Run down to the kitchen, dearie," said Martha. Her cheeks were flushed. She was carrying a big can of steaming water. "You must keep very, *very* quiet this evening and go to bed like a good boy, and perhaps to-morrow morning I'll tell you a great, great secret." She kissed me with hasty rapture. I was not especially inquisitive of her secret just then, and eagerly promised to be quite quiet if I might continue to play where I was.

'"Well, very, *very* quiet then, and you mustn't let Mrs Marshall," she began, but hurried hastily away in answer to a peremptory summons from upstairs.

'Almost as soon as she was gone I heard a light rap on the door. It seemed that Jane Grey had brought in with her the cold and freshness of the woods. I led the way on tiptoe down the narrow corridor and into the small, silent room. The candles burned pure and steadfastly in their brightness. The air was still and languid with the perfume of flowers. Overhead passed light, heedful footsteps; but they seemed not a disturbing sound, only a rumour beyond the bounds of silence.

'"I am very sorry," I said, "but they have nailed it down. Martha says the men came this afternoon."

'Miss Grey took a little bunch of snowdrops from her bosom, and hid them in among the clustered wreaths of flowers; and she knelt down on the floor, with a little silver cross which she sometimes wore pressed tight to her lips. I felt ill at ease to see her praying, and wished I could go back to my soldiers. But while I watched her, seeing in marvellous brilliancy everything in the little room, and remembering dimly the snow lying beneath the stars in the darkness of the garden, I listened also to the quiet footsteps passing to and fro in the room above. Suddenly, the silence was broken by a small, continuous, angry crying.

'Miss Grey looked up. Her eyes were very clear and wonderful in the candlelight.

'"What was that?" she said faintly, listening.

'I stared at her. The cry welled up anew, piteously; as if of a small remote and helpless indignation.

'"Why it sounds just like a – little baby," I said.

'She crossed herself hastily and arose. "Nicholas!" she said in a strange, quiet, bewildered voice – yet her face was most curiously bright. She looked at me lovingly and yet so strangely I wished I had not let her come in.

'She went out as she had entered. I did not so much as peep into the darkness after her, but busy with a hundred thoughts, returned to my play.

'Long past my usual bedtime, as I sat sipping a mug of hot milk before the glowing cinders of the kitchen fire, Martha told me her secret…

'So my impossible companion in the High Street yesterday was own, and only brother to your crazy old friend, Richard,' said the Count. 'His only brother,' he added, in a muse.

Crewe

When murky winter dusk begins to settle over the railway station at Crewe its first-class waiting-room grows steadily more stagnant. Particularly if one is alone in it. The long grimed windows do little more than sift the failing light that slopes in on them from the glass roof outside and is too feeble to penetrate into the recesses beyond. And the grained massive black-leathered furniture becomes less and less inviting. It appears to have been made for a scene of extreme and diabolical violence that one may hope will never occur. One can hardly at any rate imagine it to have been designed by a really *good* man!

Little things like this of course are apt to become exaggerated in memory, and I may be doing the Company an injustice. But whether this is so or not – and the afternoon I have in mind is now many years distant – I certainly became more acutely conscious of the defects of my surroundings when the few fellow-travellers who had been sharing this dreadful apartment with me had hurried out at the clang of a bell for the down train, leaving me to wait for the up. And nothing and nobody, as I supposed, but a great drowsy fire of cinders in the iron grate for company.

The almost animated talk that had sprung up before we parted, never in this world to meet again, had been occasioned by an account in the morning's newspapers of the last voyage of a ship called the *Hesper*. She had come in the evening before, and some days overdue, with a cargo of sugar from the West Indies, and was now berthed safely in the Southampton Docks. This seemed to have been something of a relief to those concerned. For even her master had not refused to admit that certain mysterious and tragic events had recently occurred on board, though he preferred not to discuss them with a reporter. He agreed, even with the reporter, however, that there had been a full moon at the time, that, apart from a heavy swell, the sea was 'as calm as a mill-pond', and that his ship was at present in want of a second mate. But the voyage of the *Hesper* is now, of course, an old tale many times told. And I myself, having taken very little part in the discussion, had by that time wearied of her mysteries and had decided to seek the lights and joys and coloured bottles of the refreshment room when a voice from out of the murk behind me suddenly broke the hush. It was an unusual voice, rapid, incoherent and internal, like that of a man in a dream or under the influence of a drug.

I shifted my high-backed ungainly chair and turned to look. Evidently this, the only other occupant of the room, had until that moment been as unaware of my presence in it as I of his. Indeed he seemed to have been completely taken aback at finding he was not alone. He had started up from out of his obscure corner beyond the high window and was staring across at me out of his flat greyish face in unconcealed stupefaction. He seemed for a moment or two to be in doubt even of what I was. Then he sighed, a sigh that ended in a long shuddering yawn. 'I am sorry,' I said, 'I supposed – '

But he interrupted me – and not as if my company, now that he had recognized me as a fellow creature, was any the less welcome for being unexpected.

'Merely what I was saying, sir,' he was mildly explaining, 'is that those gentlemen there who have just left us had no more notion of what they were talking about than an infant in the cradle.'

This elegant paraphrase, I realized, bore only the feeblest resemblance to the violent soliloquy I had just overheard. I looked at him. 'How so?' I said. 'I am only a landsman myself, but... '

It had seemed unnecessary to finish the sentence – I have never seen anyone less marine in effect than *he* was. He had shifted a little nearer and was now, his legs concealed, sitting on the extreme edge of his vast wooden sofa – a smallish man, but muffled up in a very respectable greatcoat at least two sizes too large for him, his hands thrust deep into its pockets.

He continued to stare at me. 'You don't have to go to sea for things like that,' he went on. 'And there's no need to argue about it if you do. Still it wasn't my place to interfere. They'll find out all right – all in good time. They go their ways. And talking of that, now, have you ever heard say that there is less risk sitting in a railway carriage at sixty miles an hour than in laying alone, safe, as you might suppose, in your own bed? That's true, too.' He glanced round him. 'You know where you are in a place like this, too. It's solid, though – ' I couldn't catch the words that followed, but they seemed to be uncomplimentary to things in general.

'Yes,' I agreed, 'it certainly looks solid.'

'Ah, "looks",' he went on cantankerously. 'But what *is* your "solid", come to that? I thought so myself once.' He seemed to be pondering over the *once*. 'But now', he added, 'I know different.'

With that he rose and, dwarfed a little perhaps by the length of his coat, sallied out of his obscure corner beyond the high window and came to the fire. After warming his veined shrunken hands at the heap of smouldering cinders in the grate under the black marble mantelpiece – he seated himself opposite to me.

At risk of seeming fastidious, I must confess that now he was near I did not much care for the appearance of this stranger. He might be about to solicit a small loan. In spite of his admirable greatcoat he looked in need of a barber, as well as of medicine and sleep – a need that might presently exhibit itself in a hankering for alcohol. But I was mistaken. He asked for nothing, not even sympathy, not even advice. He merely, it seemed, wanted to talk about himself. And perhaps a complete stranger makes a better receptacle for a certain kind of confidences than one's intimates. He tells no tales.

Nevertheless I shall attempt to tell Mr Blake's, and as far as possible in his own peculiar idiom. It impressed me at the time. And I have occasionally speculated since whether his statistics in relation to the risks of railway travel proved trustworthy. *Safety first* is a sound principle so far as it goes, but we are all of us out-manoeuvred in the end. And I still wonder what end was his.

He began by asking me if I had ever lived in the country – 'In the depps of the country'. And then, quickly realizing that I was more inclined to listen than talk, he suddenly plunged into his past. It seemed to refresh him to do so.

'I was a gentleman's servant when I began,' he set off; 'first boot-boy under a valet, then footman and helping at table, then pantry work and so on. Never married or anything of that; petti-coats are nothing but encumbrances in the house. But I must say if you keep yourself *to* yourself, it sees you through – in time. What you have to beware of is those of your own calling. Domestic. That's the same everywhere; nobody's reached much past the cat-and-dog stage in that. Not if you look close enough; high or low. I lost one or two nice easy places all on that account. Jealousy. And if you don't stay where you are put there's precious little chance of pickings when the funeral's at the door. But that's mostly changed, so I'm told; high wages and no work being the order of the day; and gratitude to follow suit. They are all rolling stones nowadays, and never mind the moss.'

As a philosopher this white-faced muffled-up old creature seemed to affect realism, though his reservations on the 'solid' had fallen a little short of it. Not that *my* reality appeared to matter much – beyond, I mean the mere proof of it. For though in the rather intimate memories he proceeded to share with me he frequently paused to ask a question, he seldom waited for an answer, and then ignored it. I see now this was not to be won-dered at. We happened to be sharing at the moment this – for my part – chance resort and he wanted company – human company.

'The last situation I was in' (he was going on to tell me), 'was with the Reverend W. Somers, M.A.: William. In the depps of the country, as I say. Just myself, a young fellow of the name of George, and a woman who came in from the village to char and cook and so on, though I did the best part of that myself. The finishing touches, I mean. How long the Reverend hadn't cared for females in the house I never knew; but parsons have their share of them, I'm thinking. Not that he wasn't attached enough to his sister. They had grown up together, nursery to drawing-room, and that covers a multitude of sins.

'Like *him*, *she* was, but more of the parrot in appearance; a high face with a beaky nose. Quite a nice lady, too, except that she was mighty slow in being explained to. No interference, generally speaking; in spite of her nose. But don't mistake me; we had to look alive when she was in the house. Oh, yes. But that, thank God, was seldom. And in the end it made no difference.

'She never took to the Vicarage. Who would? I can hear her now – Blake this, and Blake that. Too dark, too vaulty, too shut in. And in winter freezing cold, laying low maybe. Trees in front, everlastings; though open behind with a stream and cornfields and hills in the distance; especially in summer, of course. They went up and down, and dim and dark, according to the weather. You could see for miles from those upper corridor windows – small panes that take a lot of cleaning. But George did the windows. George had come from the village, too, if you could call it a village. But he was a permanency. Nothing much but a few cottages, and an outlying farmhouse here and there. Why the old brick church lay about a mile away from it, I can't say. To give the Roaring Lion a trot, perhaps. The Reverend had private means – naturally. I knew that before it came out in the will. But it was a nice fat living notwith-standing – worked out at about fifty pounds to the pig-sty,

I shouldn't wonder, with the vicarage thrown in. You get what you've got in this world, and some of us enjoy a larger slice than we deserve. But the Reverend, I must say, never took advantage of it. He was a gentleman. Give him his books, and to-morrow like yesterday, and he gave no trouble – none whatever.

'Mind you, he liked things as they should be, and he had some of the finest silver I ever lay finger on; and old furniture to match. I don't mean furniture picked up at sales and such like, but real old family stuff. That's where the parrot in the family nose came from. Everything punctual to the minute and the good things *good*. Soup or fish, a cutlet, a savoury, and a glass of sherry or madeira. No sweets – though he was a lean, spare gentleman, silvery beard and all. And I have never seen choicer fruit than came from his houses and orchard, though it was here the trouble began. Cherries, gages, peaches, nectarines – old red sun-baked walls nine or ten feet high and a sight like wonder in the spring. I used to go out specially to have a look at them. He had his fancies, too, had the Reverend. If any smoking was to be done it must be in the shrubbery with the blackbirds, not under the roof. And sitting there in his study, sir, he could detect the whiff of a cigarette even in the furthest of the attics!

'But tobacco's not *my* trouble, never was. Keep off what you don't need, and you won't want it when you can't get it. That's my feeling. It was, as I say, an easy place, if you forgot how quiet it was – not a sound, no company, and not a soul to be seen. Fair prospects, too, if you could wait. He had no fancy for change, had the Reverend; made no concealment of it. He told me himself that he had remembered me in his will – "if still in his service". You know how these lawyers put it. As a matter of fact he had given me to understand that if in the meantime for any reason any of us went elsewhere, the one left was to have the lot. But not death. *There*, as it turned out, I was in error.

'But I'm not complaining of that now. He was a gentleman; and I have enough to see me through however long I'm left. And that might be for a good many years yet.'

The intonation of this last remark suggested a question. But my confidant made no pause for an answer and added argumentatively, 'Who *wants* to go, I should like to ask? Early or late. And nothing known of what's on the other side?' He lifted his grey eyebrows a little as if to glance up at me as he sat stooped up by the fire, and yet refrained from doing so. And again I couldn't enlighten him.

'Well, there, as I say, I might have stayed to this day if the old gentleman's gardener had cared to stay too. *He* began it. Him gone, we all went. Like ninepins. You might hardly credit it, sir, but I am the only one left of that complete establishment. Gutted. And that's where these fine gentlemen here were talking round their hats. What I say is, keep on this side of the tomb as long as you can. Don't meddle with that hole. Why? Because while some fine day you will have to go down into it, you can never be quite sure while you are here what mayn't come back out of it.

'*There'll be no partings there* – I have heard them trolling that out in them chapels like missel-thrushes in the spring. They seem to forget there may be some mighty unpleasant *meetings*. And what about the further shore? It's my belief there's some kind of a ferry plying on that river. And coming back depends on what you want to come back *for*.

'Anyhow the Vicarage reeked of it. A low old house, with lots of little windows and far too many doors; and, as I say, the trees too close up on one side, almost brushing the glass. No wonder they said it was what they call haunted. You could feel that with your eyes shut, and like breeds like. The Vicar – two or three, I mean, before my own gentleman – had even gone to the trouble of having the place exercised. Candles and holy water, that kind of thing. Sheer flummummery, *I* call it. But if what I've heard there – and long before that gowk of a George came to work in the house – was anything more than mere age and owls and birds in the ivy, it must badly have needed it. And when you get accustomed to noises, you can tell which from which. By usual, I mean. Though more and more I'm getting to ask myself if any thing is anything much more than what you think it is – for the time being.

'Same with noises of course. What's this voice of conscience that they talk about but something you needn't hear if you don't want to? I am not complaining of that. If at the beginning there was anything in that house that was better out than in, it never troubled me; at least, not at first. And the Reverend, even though you could often count his congregation on your ten fingers, except at Harvest Festival, was so wove up in his books that I doubt if he'd have been roused up out of 'em even by the Last Trump. It's my belief that in those last few weeks – when I stepped in to see to the fire – as often as not he was sitting asleep over them.

'No, I'm not complaining. Live at peace with who you can, I say. But when it comes to as crusty a customer, and a Scotchman at that, as was my friend the gardener, then there's a limit. Mengus he called himself, though I can't see *how*, if you spell it with a z. When I first came into the place it was all gold that glitters. I'm not the man for contentiousness, if let alone. But afterwards, when the rift came, I don't suppose we ever hardly exchanged the time of day but what there came words of it. A long-legged man *he* was, this Mr Menzies; too long I should have thought for strict comfort in grubbing and hoeing and weeding. He had ginger hair, scanty, and the same on his face, whiskers – and a stoop. He lived down at the lodge; and his widowed daughter kept house for him, with one little boy as fair as she was dark. Harmless enough as children go, the kind they call an angel, but noisy, and not for the house.

'Now why, I ask you, shouldn't I pick a little of this gentleman's precious fruit, or a cucumber for a salad, if need be, and him not there? What if I wanted a few grapes for dessert or a nice apricot tart for the Reverend's luncheon, and our Mr Menzies gone home or busy with the frames? I don't hold with all these hard and fast restrictions, at least outside the house. Not he, though! We wrangled about it week in, week out. And him with a temper which once roused was past all reasoning.

'Not that I ever took much notice of him until it came to a point past any man's enduring. I let him rave. But duty is duty, there's no getting away from that. And when, apart from all this fuss about his fruit, a man takes advantage of what is meant in pure friendliness, well, one's bound to make a move. Job himself.

'What I mean to say is, I used occasionally – window wide open and all that, the pantry being on the other side of the house and away from the old gentleman's study – I say I used occasionally, and all in the way of friendliness, to offer our friend a drink. Like as with many of Old Adam's trade, drink was a little weakness of his, though I don't mean I hold with it because of that. But peace and quietness is the first thing, and to keep an easy face to all appearances, even if you do find it a little hard at times to forgive and forget.

'When he was civil, as I say, and as things should be, he could have a drink, and welcome. When not, not. But it came to become a kind of habit; and to be expected; which is always a bad condition of things. Oh, it was a thousand pities! There was the Reverend, growing feeble as you could see, and him believing all the while that everything around him was calm and sweet as the new Jerusalem, while there was nothing but strife and agrimony, as they call it, underneath. There's many a house looks as snug and cosy as a nut. But crack it and look inside! Mildew. Still, our Mr Mengus had "prospects," up to then.

'Well, there came along at last a mighty hot summer – five years ago, you may remember. Five years ago, next August, an extraordinary hot summer. And an early harvest – necessarily. Day after day I could see the stones in the stubble fields shivering in the sun. And gardening is thirsty work; I will say that for it. Which being so, better surely virgin water from the tap or a drop of cider, same as the harvesters have, than ardent spirits, whether it is what you are bred up to or not! It stands to reason.

'Besides, we had had words again, and though I can stretch a point with a friend and no harm done, I'm not a man to come coneying and currying favour. Let him get his own drinks, was my feeling in the matter. And you can hardly call me to blame if he did. *There* was the pantry window hanging wide open in the shade of the trees – and day after day of scorching sun and not a breath to breathe. And there was the ruin of him within arm's reach from outside, and a water tap handy, too. Very inviting, I'll allow.

'I'm not attesting, mind you, that he was confirmed at it, no more than that I'm a man to be measuring what's given me to take charge of by tenths of inches. It's the principle of the thing. You might have thought, too, that a simple honest pride would have kept him back. Nothing of the sort; and no matter, wine or spirits. I'd watch him there, though he couldn't see me, being behind the door. And practices like that, sir, as you will agree with me, can't go on. They couldn't go on, vicarage or no vicarage. Besides, from being secret it began to be open. It had gone too far. Brazen it out: that was the lay. I came down one fine morning to find one of my best decanters smashed to smithereens on the stone floor, Irish glass and all. Cats and sherry, who ever heard of it? And out of revenge he filled the pantry with wasps by bringing in over-ripe plums. Petty waste of time like that. And some of the green-houses thick with blight!

'And so things went, from bad to worse, and at such a pace as I couldn't have credited. A widower, too, with a married daughter dependent on him; which is worse even than a wife, who expects to take the bad with the good. No, sir, I had to call a halt to it. A friendly word in his ear, or keeping everything out of his reach, you may be thinking, might have sufficed. Believe me, not for him. And how can you foster such a weakness by taking steps out of the usual to prevent it? It wouldn't be proper to your self-respect. Then I thought of George; not com*prom*ising myself in any way, of course, in so doing. George had a face as long as your arm, pale and solemn, enough to make a cat laugh. Dress him up in a surplice and hassock, he might have been the Reverend's curate. Strange that, for a youth born in the country. But curate or no curate, he had eyes in his head and must have seen what there was to be seen.

'I said to him one day, and I remember him standing there in the pantry in his black coat against the white of the cupboard paint, I said to him, "George, a word in time saves nine, but it would come better from you than from me. You take me? Hold your peace till our friend's sober again and can listen to reason. Then hand it over to him – a word of warning, I mean. Say we are muffling things up as well as we *can* from the old gentleman, but that if he should hear of it there'd be fat in the fire; and no mistake. He would take it easier from you, George, the responsibility being mine."

'Lord, how I remember George! He had a way of looking at you as if he couldn't say *Boh* to a goose – swollen hands and bolting blue eyes, as simple as an infant's. But he wasn't stupid, oh no. Nobody could say that. And now I reflect, I think he knew our little plan wouldn't carry very far. But there, whatever he might be thinking, he was so awkward with his tongue that he could never find anything to say until it was too late, so I left it at that. Besides, I had come to know he was, with all his faults, a young man you could trust for doing what he was told to do. So, as I say, I left it at that.

'What he actually did say I never knew. But as for its being of any use, it was more like pouring paraffin on a bonfire. The very next afternoon our friend came along to the pantry window and stood there looking in – swaying he was, on his feet; and I can see the midges behind him zigzagging in a patch of sunshine as though they were here before my very eyes. He was so bad that he had to lay hold of the sill to keep himself from falling. Not thirst this time, but just fury. And then, seeing that mere flaunting of fine feathers wasn't going to inveigle *me* into a cockfight, he began to talk. Not all bad language, mind you – *that's* easy to shut your ears to – but cold reasonable abuse, which isn't. At first I took no notice, went on about my business at my leisure, and no hurry. What's the use of arguing with a man, and him one of these Scotchmen to boot, that's beside himself with rage? What was wanted was *peace* in the house, if only for the old gentleman's sake, who I thought was definitely under the weather and had been coming on very poorly of late.

'"Where's that George of yours?" he said to me at last – with additions. "Where's that George? Fetch him out, and I'll teach him to come playing the holy Moses to my own daughter. Fetch him out, I say, and we'll finish it here and now." And all pitched high, and half his words no more English than the mewing of a cat.

'But I kept my temper and answered him quite moderate and as pleasantly as I knew how. "I don't want to meddle in *any*body's quarrels," I said. "So long as George so does his work in this house as will satisfy *my* eye, I am not responsible for his actions in his off-time and out of bounds."

'How was I to know, may I ask, if it was *not* our Mr Mengus who had smashed one of my best decanters? What proof was there? What *reason* had I for thinking else?

'"George is a quiet, unbeseeming young fellow," I said, "and if he thinks it's his duty to report any misgoings-on either to me or to the Reverend, it doesn't concern anybody else."

'That seemed to sober my fine gentleman. Mind you, I'm not saying that there was anything unremidibly wrong with him. He was a first-class gardener. I grant you that. But then he had an uncommonly good place to match – first-class wages; and no milk, wood, coals or house-rent to worry about. But breaking out like that, and the Reverend poorly and all; that's not what he thought of when he put us all down in his will. I'll be bound of that. Well, there he stood, looking in at the window and me behind the table in my apron as calm as if his wrangling meant no more to me than the wind in the chimmeny. It was the word "report", I fancy, that took the wind out of his sails. It had brought him up like a station buffer. And he was still looking at me, and brooding it over, as though he had the taste of poison on his tongue.

'Then he says very quiet, "So that's his little game, is it? You are just a pair, then?"

'"If by pair you're meaning me," I said, "well, I'm ready to take my share of the burden when it's ready to fit my back. But not before. George may have gone a bit beyond himself, but he meant well, and you know it."

'"What I am asking is this," says our friend, "have you ever seen me the worse for liquor? Answer me that!"

'"If I liked your tone better," I said, "I wouldn't say how I don't see why it would be necessarily the *worse*."

'"Ehh? You mean, Yes, then?" he said.

'"I mean no more than what I say," I answered him, looking at him over the cruet as straight as I'm looking at you now. "I don't ask to meddle with your private affairs, and I'll thank *you* not to come meddling with mine." He seemed taken aback at that, and I noticed he was looking a bit pinched, and hollow under the eyes. Sleepless nights, perhaps.

'But how was *I* to know this precious grandson of his was out of sorts with a bad throat and that – seeing that he hadn't mentioned it till a minute before? I ask you! "The best thing you and George there can do," I went on, "is to bury the hatchet; and out of hearing of the house, too."

'With that I turned away and went off into it myself, leaving him there to think things over at his leisure. I am putting it to you, sir, as a free witness, what else could I have done?'

There was little light of day left in our cavernous waiting-room by this time. Only the dulling glow of the fire and the phosphorescence caused by a tiny bead of gas in the 'mantles' of the great iron bracket over our heads. My realist seemed to be positively in want of an answer to this last question. But as I sat looking back into his intent small face nothing that could be described as of a helpful nature offered itself.

'If he was anxious about his grandson,' I ventured at last, 'it might explain his being a little short in temper. Besides… But I should like to hear what came after.'

'What came after, now?' the little man repeated, drawing his right hand gingerly out of the depths of his pocket and smoothing down his face with it as if he had suddenly discovered he was tired. 'Well, a good deal came after, but not quite what you might have expected. And you'd hardly go so far as to say perhaps that anxiety over his grandson would excuse him for what was little short of manslaughter, and him a good six inches to the good at that? Keeping facts as facts, if you'll excuse me, our friend waylaid George by the stables that very evening, and a wonderful peaceful evening it was, shepherd's delight and all that. But to judge from the looks of the young fellow's face when he came into the house there hadn't been much of that in the quarter of an hour they had had together.

'I said, "Sponge it down, George, sponge it down. And by good providence maybe the old gentleman won't notice anything wrong." It wasn't to reason I could let him off his duties and enter into a lot of silly peravications which in the long run might only make things worse. It's that you have to think of when you are a man in my position. But as for the Reverend's not noticing it, there, as luck would have it, I was wrong myself.

'For when the two of us were leaving the dining-room that evening after the table had been cleared and the dessert put on, he looked up from round the candles and told George to stay behind. Some quarter of an hour after that George came along to me snuffling as if he'd been crying. But I asked no questions, not me; and, as I say, he was always pretty slow with his tongue. All that I could get out of him was that he had decocted some cock-and-bull story to account for his looks the like of which nobody in his senses could credit, let alone such a power of questioning as the old gentleman could bring to bear when roused, and apart from what comes, I suppose, from reading so many books. So the fat was in the fire and no mistake. And the next thing I heard, after coming back late the following evening, was that our Mr Mengus had been called into the house and given the sack there and then, with a quarter's wages in lieu of notice. Which, after all, mind you, was as good as three-quarters a gift. What I'm saying is that handsome is as handsome does, and that was the Reverend all over; though I agree, mind you, even money isn't necessarily everything when there's what they call character to be taken into account. But if ever there was one of the quality fair and upright in all his dealings, as the saying goes, then that was the Reverend Somers. And I abide by that. He wouldn't have any truck with drink topped with insolence. That's all.

'Well, our friend came rapping at the back door that evening, shaken to the marrow if ever man was, and just livid. I told him, and I meant it too, that I was sorry for what had occurred: "It's a bad ending", I said, "to a tale that ought never to have been told." I told him too, speaking as quiet and pleasant as I am to you now, that the only hope left was to let bygones be bygones; that he had already had his fingers on George, and better go no further. Not he. He said, and he was sober enough then in all conscience, that, come what come may, here or hereafter, he'd be even with him. Ay, and he made mention of me also, but not so rabid. A respectable man, too; never a word against him till then; and not far short of sixty. And by rabid I don't mean violent. He spoke as low and quiet as if there was a judge on the bench there to hear him, sentence said and everything over. And then… '

The old creature paused until yet another main-line train had gone roaring on its way. 'And then,' he continued, 'though he wasn't found till morning, he must have gone straight out – and good-bye said to nobody. He must, I say, have gone straight out to the old barn and hanged himself. The midmost rafter, sir, and a drop that would have sufficed for a Giant Goliath. All night. And it's my belief, good-bye or no good-bye, that it wasn't so much the *disgrace* of the affair but his daughter – Mrs Shaw by name – and his grandson that were preying on his mind. And yet – why, he never so much as asked me to say a good word for him! Not one.

'Well, that was the end of that. So far. And it's a curious thing to me – though they say these Romans aren't above making use of it – how, going back over the past clears everything up like; at least for the time being. But it's what you were saying just now about what's *solid* that sets me thinking and keeps repeating itself in my mind. Solid was the word you used. And they look it, I agree.' He deliberately twisted his head and fastened a prolonged stare on the bench on which he had been seated. 'But it doesn't follow there's much comfort in them even if they are.

Solid or not, they go at last when all's said to what's little else but gas and ashes once they're fallen to pieces and been put on the fire. Which holds good, and even more so, for them that sit on them. Peculiar habit that, too – sitting! Yes, I've been told, sir, that after what they call this cremation, and all the moisture in us gone up in steam, what's left would scarcely turn the scales by a single *hounce!*'

If sitting *is* a peculiar habit, it was even more peculiar how etherealizing the effect of my new acquaintance's misplaced aspirate had been – his one and only lapse in this respect throughout his interminable monologue.

'Yes, they say that so far as this *solid* goes, we amount to no more than what you could put into a walnut. And my point, sir,' he was emphasizing with a forefinger that only just showed itself beyond the long sleeve of his greatcoat, 'my point is *this* – that if *that's* all there is to you and me, we shouldn't need much of the substantial for what you might call the mere sole look of things, if you follow me, if *we* chose or chanced to come back. When gone, I mean. Just enough, I suppose, to be obnoxious, as the Reverend used to say, to the naked eye.

'But all that being as it may be, the whole thing had tided over, and George was pretty nearly himself again, and another gardener advertised for – and I must say the Reverend, though after this horrible affair he was never the same man again, treated the young woman I mentioned as if he himself had been a father – I say, the whole thing had tided over, and the house was as silent as a tomb again, ay, as the sepulchre itself, when I began to notice something peculiar.

'At first maybe, little more *than* mere silence. What, in the contrast, as a matter of fact, I took for *peace*. But afterwards not so. There was a strain, so to speak, as you went about your daily doings. A strain. And especially after dark. It may have been only in one's head. I can't say. But it was there: and I could see without watching that even George had noticed it, and *he'd* hardly notice a black-beetle on a pancake.

'And at last there came something you could put word to, catch in the act, so to speak. I had gone out towards the cool of the evening after a broiling hot day, to get a little air. There was a copse of beeches, which as perhaps you may know, is a very pleasant tree for shade, sir, at a spot a bit under the mile from the back of the Vicarage. And I sat there quiet for a minute or two, with the birds and all – they were beginning to sing again, I remember – and – you know how memory strays back, though sometimes it's more like a goat tethered to a peg on a common – I was thinking over what a curious thing it is how one man's poison is another man's meat. For the funeral over, and all that, the old gentleman had thanked me for all I had done. You see what had gone before had been a hard break in his trust of a man, and he looked up from his bed at me almost with tears in his eyes. He said he wouldn't forget it. He used the word substantial, sir; and I ought by rights to have mentioned that he was taken ill the night of the inquest; a sort of stroke, the doctor called it, though he came round, I must say, remarkably well considering his age.

'Well, I had been thinking over all this on the fringe of the woods there, and was on my way back again to the house by the field-path, when I looked up as if at call and saw what I take my oath I never remembered to have seen there before – a scarecrow. A scarecrow – and that right in the middle of the cornfield that lay beyond the stream with the bulrushes at the back of the house. Nothing funny in that, you may say. Quite so. But mark me, this was early September, and the stubble all bleaching in the sun, and it didn't look an *old* scarecrow, either. It stood up with its arms out and an old hat down over its eyes, bang in the middle of the field, its back to me, and its front to the house. I knew that field as well as I know my own face in the looking-glass. Then how could I have missed it? What wonder then I stood stock still and had a good long stare at it, first because, as I say, I had never seen it before, and next because – but I'll be coming to that later.

'That done, and *not* to my satisfaction, I turned back a little and came along on the other side of the hedge, and so, presently at last, indoors. Then I stepped up to the upper storey to have a look at it from the windows. For you never know with these country people what they are up to, though they may seem stupid enough. Looked at from there, it wasn't so much in the middle of the field as I had fancied, seeing it from the other side. But how, thought I to myself, could you have escaped me, my friend, if you had been there all through the summer? I don't see how it could; that's flat. But if not, then it must have been put up more recently.

'I had all but forgotten about it next morning, but as afternoon came on I went upstairs and had another look. There was less heat-haze or something, and I could see it clearer and nearer, so to speak, but not quite clear enough. So I whipped along to the Reverend's study, him being still, poor gentleman, confined to his bed. In fact he never got up from it; I whipped along, I say, to the study to fetch his glasses, his boniculars, and I fastened them on that scarecrow like a microscope on a fly. You will hardly credit me, sir, when I say that what seemed to me then most different about it – different from what you might expect – was that it didn't look in any ordinary manner of speaking, quite *real*.

'I could watch it with the glasses as plain as if it had been in touch of my hand, even to the buttons and the hat-band. It wasn't the first time I had set eyes on the *clothes*, either, though I couldn't have laid name to them. And there was something in the appearance of the thing, something in the way it bore itself up, so to speak, with its arms thrown up at the sky and its empty face, which wasn't what you'd expect of mere sticks and rags. Not, I mean, if they were nothing but just real – real like that there chair, I mean, you are sitting on now.

'I called George. I said, "George, lay your eye to these glasses" – and his face was still a bit discoloured, though his little affair in the stableyard was now a good three weeks old. "Take a squint through these, George," I said, "and tell me what you make of *that* thing over there."

'George was a slow dawdling mug if ever there was one – clumsy-fingered. But he fixed the glasses at last, and he took a good long look. Then he gave them back into my hand.

'"Well?" I said, watching his face.

'"Why, Mr Blake," he said, meaning me, "it's a scarecrow."

'"How would you like it a bit nearer?" I said. Just off-hand, like that.

'He looked at me. "It's near enough in *them*," he said.

'"Does the air round it strike you as funny at all?" I asked him. "Out-of-the-way funny – *quivering*, in a manner of speaking?"

'"That's the heat," he said, but his lip trembled.

'"Well, George," I said, "heat or no heat, you or me must go and have a look at that thing closer some time. But not this after-noon. It's too late."

'But we didn't, sir, neither me *nor* him, though I fancy he went on thinking about it on his own account in between. And lo and behold, when I got up next morning and had slid out of my bedroom early, and went along into the corridor to have another glance at it, and – believe me, sir, as you looked out into the morning the country lay as calm and open as a map – it wasn't there. The scarecrow, sir. It wasn't there. It was vanished. Nor could I get a glimpse of it from downstairs through the bushes *this* side of the stream. And all so still and early that even there from the back door you could hear the water moving. Now who, thinks I to myself, is answerable for *this* jiggery-pokery?

'But it's no good in this world, sir, putting reasons more far-fetched to a thing than are necessary to account for it. That you *will* agree. Some farmer's lout, I thought to myself, must have come and moved the old mommet overnight. But, that being so, what was it ever put up for? Harvest done, mind you, and the crows, one would think, as welcome to what they could pick up in the stubble – if they hadn't picked it all up already – as robins to house crumbs. Besides, what about the peculiar looks of it?

'I didn't go out next day, not at all; and there being only George and me in the Vicarage, and the Reverend shut off in his room, I never remember such a holy quiet. The heavens like a vault. Eighty-four in the shade by the thingamy in the verandah and this the fourth of September. All day long, and I'll vouch for it, the whole twenty acres of that field, but for the peewits and the rooks running over it, lay empty. And when, the sun going down, the harvest moon came up that evening – and that summer she showed up punctual as a clock the whole month round – you could see right across the flat country to the hills. And the night-jars croaking too. You could have cut the heat with a knife.

'What time the old gentleman's gruel was gone up and George out of the way, I took yet another squint through the glasses from the upper windows. And I am ready to own that something inside of me gave a sort of a *hump*, sir, when, large as life, I saw that the scarecrow was come back again, though this is where you'll have, if you please, to go careful with me. What I saw the instant before I began to look, and to that I'd lay my affidavit, was something moving, and pretty rapid, too; and it was only at the very moment I clapped the glasses on to it that it suddenly fixed itself into what I already *supposed* I should find it to be. I've noticed that – though in little things not mattering much – before. It's your own mind that learns you before what you look at turns out to be what you expect. Else why should we be alarmed by this here *solid* sometimes? It *looks* all so; but *is* it?

'You might be suggesting that both shape and scarecrow too were all my eye and Betty Martin. But we'll see later on about that. And what about George? You don't mean to infer that he could borrow to order a mere fancy clean out of my head and turn it into a scarecrow in the middle of a field and in broad daylight too? That would be the long bow, and no mistake. Ay, and take it in some shape for what we *did!* No. Yet, as I say, even when I first cast eyes on it, it looked too real to be real. So there's the two on the one side, and the two on the other, and they don't make four.

'Well, sir, I must say that from that moment on I didn't like the look of things, and never have I shared a meal so mum as when George and me sat to supper that evening. From being a hearty eater his appetite was fallen almost to a cipher. He munched and couldn't swallow. I doubt if his vittles had a taste of them left. And we both of us knew as though it had been printed on the tablecloth what the other was thinking about.

'It was while we sat there, George and me alone, him on the right and the window opposite, and me on the cupboard side in what was called the servants' hall, that we heard some words said. Not what you could understand, but still, words. I couldn't tell from where, except that it wasn't from the Reverend, and I couldn't tell what. But they dropped upon us and between us as if there was a parrot in the room, clapping its horny bill, so to say, motionless in the air. At this George stopped munching for good, his face little short of green. But except for a cockling up inside of me, I didn't make any sign I'd heard. After all, it was nothing that made any difference to *me*, though what was going on was, to say the least of it, not all as it should be. And if you knew the old Vicarage you'd agree.

'Lock-up time came at last. And George took his candle and went up to bed. Not quite as willing as usual, I fancied; though he had always been a glutton for his full meed of sleep. You could notice by the sound of his feet on the stairs that he was as you might say pushing of himself on. As for me, it had always been my way to sit up after him reading a bit with the Reverend's *Times*. But that night, I went off early. I gave a last look in on the old gentleman, and I might as well mention – though dilatory isn't the word for these doctors, even when they *are* called in in reasonable time – I say a nurse had been sent for, and his sister was now expected any day from Scotland. All well there, and him lying as peaceful on his bed as if the end had come already. Well, sir, that done, coming back along the corridor I blew out my candle and stood waiting. The candle out, the moon came streaming in, and the outside from the window lay spread out beneath me almost bright as day. I looked this ways and I looked that ways, back and front; but nothing to be seen, nor heard neither. Yet it seemed not more than one deep breath after I had closed my eyes in sleep that night that I was stark wideawake again, trying to make sense of some sound I'd heard.

'Old houses – I'm used to them; the timbers crinkle like a bee-hive. But this wasn't timbers, oh no! It might maybe have been wind, you'll say. But what chance of wind with not a hand's breadth of cloud moving in the sky, and such a blare of moon-light as would keep even a field mouse from peeping out of its hole? What's more, not to know whether what you are listening to is in or outside of your head isn't much help to a good night's rest. Still I fell off at last, unnoticing.

'Next morning, as George came back from taking up the breakfast tray, I had a good look at him in the sunlight, but you couldn't tell whether the marks round his eyes were natural – from what had gone before with the other, I mean – or from *insommia*. Best not to meddle, I thought; just wait. So I gave him good morning and poured out the coffee and we sat to it as usual, the wasps coming in over the marmalade as if nothing had happened.

'All quiet that day, only rather more so, as it always is in a sick-room house. Doctor come and gone, but no nurse yet; and the old gentleman I thought looking very ailing. But he spoke to me quite cheerful. Just like his old self, too, to be sympathizing with me for the double-duty I'd been doing in the house. He asked after the garden, too, though there was as fine a bunch of black grapes on his green plate as any out of Canaan. It was the drought was in his mind. And just as I was leaving the room, my hand on the door, he mentioned one or two compliments about my having stayed on with him so long. "You can't pay for that out of any Bank," he said to me, smiling at me almost merry-like, his beard over the sheet.

'"I hope and trust, sir," I said, "while I am with you, there will be no further fuss." But I had a surety even as I said the words that he hadn't far to go, so that fusses, if come they did, didn't really much matter to him. I don't see how you would be likely to notice them when things are drawing to a last conclusion; though I am thankful to say that what did occur, was kept from him to the end.

'That night there came something sounding about the house that wasn't natural, and no mistake. I had scarcely slept a wink, and as soon as I heard it, I was on with my tail-coat over my night-shirt in a jiffy, though there was no need for light. I had fetched along my winter overcoat, too, one the Reverend himself had passed on to me – this very coat on my back now – and with that over my arm, I pushed open the door and looked in on George. Maybe he had heard my coming, maybe he had heard the other, I couldn't tell which, but there he was, sitting up in bed – the moonlight flooding in on his long white face and tousled hair – and his trousers and braces thrown down anyhow on the chair beside it.

'I said to him, "What's wrong, George? Did you hear anything? A voice or anything?"

'He sat looking at me with his mouth open as if he couldn't shut it, and I could see he was shaken to the very roots. Now, mind you, here I was in the same quandary, as they call it, as before. What I'd heard might be real, some animal, fox, badger, or the like, prowling round outside, or it might not. If not, and the house being exercised, as I said, though a long way back, and the Reverend gentleman still in this world himself, I had a kind of trust that what was there, if it *was* anything, couldn't get in. But naturally I was in something of a fever to make sure.

'"George," I said, "you mustn't risk a chill or anything of that sort" – and it had grown a bit cold in the small hours – "but it's up to us – our duty, George – with the Reverend at death's door and all, to know what's what. So if you'll take a look round on the outside I'll have a search through on the in. What we must be cautious about is that the old gentleman isn't disturbed."

'George went on looking at me, though he had by this time shuffled out of bed and into the overcoat I had handed him. He stood there, with his boots in his hand, shivering, but more maybe because he felt cold after the warmth of his sheets than because he had quite taken in what I had said.

'"Do you think, Mr Blake," he asked me, sitting down again on his bed, " – you don't think he is come back again?"

'*Come back*, he said, just like that. And you'd have supposed from the quivering of his mouth I might have stopped it!

'"Who's, George, come back?" I asked him.

'"Why, what we looked through the glasses at in the field," he said. "It had his look."

'"Well, George," I said, speaking as moderate and gentle as you might to a child, "we know as how dead men tell no tales.

Let alone scarecrows, then. All we've got to do is just to make sure. You do as you're bid, then, my lad. You go your ways, and I'll go mine. There's never any harm can befall a man if his conscience is easy."

'But that didn't seem to satisfy him. He gave a gulp and stood up again, still looking at me. Stupid or not, he was always one for doing his duty, was George. And I must say that what I call courage is facing what you're afraid of in your very innards, and not mere crashing into danger, eyes shut.

'"I'd lief as not go down, Mr Blake," he said. "Leastways, not alone. He never took much of a liking to me. He said he'd be evens. Not *alone*, Mr Blake."

'"What have you to fear, George, my lad?" I said. "Man or spectre, the fault was none of yours."

'He buttoned the coat up, same as I am wearing it now, and he gave me just one look more. It's hard to say all that's in a fellow-creature's eyes, sir, when they are full of what no tongue in him could tell. But George had shut his mouth at last, and the moon on his face gave him a queer look, far away-like, as if all that there was of him, this world or the next, had come to keep him company. I will say that.

'And when the hush that had come down on the house was broken again, and this time it *was* the wind, though away high up over the roof, he didn't look at me any more. It was the last between us. He turned his back on me and went off out into the passage and down the stairs, and I listened until I could hear him in the distance scrabbling with the bar at the back. It was one of those old-fashioned doors, sir, you must understand, just loaded with locks and bolts, like in all old places.

'As for myself, I didn't move for a bit. There wasn't any hurry that I could see. Oh, no. I just sat down on the bed on the place where George had sat, and waited. And you may depend upon it, I stayed pretty quiet there – with all that responsibility, and not knowing what might happen next. And then presently what I heard was as though a voice had said, something – very sharp and bitter; then said no more. There came a sort of moan, and then no more again. But by that time I was on my way on my rounds inside the house, as I'd promised; and so, out of hearing: and when I got back to my bedroom again everything was still and quiet. And I took it of course that George had got back safe to his… '

Since the fire had faded and the light of day was gone, the fish-like phosphorescence of the gas-mantles had grown brighter, and this elderly man, whose name was Blake, I understood, was looking at me out of his white, almost leper-like face in this faint gloom as steadily almost as George must have been looking at him a few minutes before he had descended the back stairs of the Vicarage, never, I gathered, to set foot on them again.

'Did you manage to get any more sleep that night?' I said.

Mr Blake seemed to be pleasingly surprised at so easy a question.

'That was the mistake of it,' he said. 'He wasn't found till morning. Cold for hours, and precious little to show why.'

'So you did manage to get a little sleep?'

But this time he made no answer.

'Your share, I suppose, was quite a substantial one?'

'Share?' he said.

'In the will…?'

'Now, didn't I tell you myself,' he protested with some warmth, 'that that, as it turned out, wasn't so; though why, it would take half a dozen or more of these lawyers to explain. And even at that, I don't know as what I did get has brought me anything much to boast about. I'm a free man, that's true. But for how long? Nobody can stay in this world here for ever, can he?'

With a peculiar rocking movement of his small head he peered round and out of the door. 'And though in this world,' he went on, 'you may have not one *iota* of harm to blame yourself for *to* yourself, there may still be misunderstandings, and them that have been deceived by them may be waiting for you in the next. So when it comes to what the captain of the *Hesper* – '

But at this moment our prolonged *tête-à-tête* was interrupted by a thickset vigorous young porter carrying a bucket of coal in one hand, and a stumpy torch of smouldering brown paper in the other. He mounted one of our chairs and with a tug of finger and thumb instantly flooded our dingy quarters with an almost intolerable gassy glare. That done, he raked out the ash-grey fire with a lump of iron that may once have been a poker, and flung all but the complete contents of his bucket of coal on to it. Then he looked round and saw who was sitting there. Me he passed over. I was merely a bird of passage. But he greeted my fellow derelict as if he were an old acquaintance.

'Good evening, sir,' he said, and in that slightly indulgent and bantering voice which suggests past favours rather easily earned. 'Let in a little light on the scene. I didn't notice you when I came in and was beginning to wonder where you had got to.'

His patron smirked back at him as if any such trifling human attention was a peculiar solace. This time the porter deliberately caught my eye. And his own was full of meaning. It was as if there were some little privy and ironical understanding between us in which this third party was unlikely to share. I ignored it, rose to my feet and clutched my bag. A passenger train had come hooting into the station, its gliding lighted windows patterning the platform planks. Alas, yet again it wasn't mine. Still – such is humanity, I preferred my own company, just then.

When I reached the door, and a cold and dingy prospect showed beyond it, I glanced back at Mr Blake, sitting there in his greatcoat beside the apparently extinguished fire. With a singularly mournful look, as of a lost dog, on his features, he was gazing after me. He seemed to be deploring the withdrawal even of my tepid companionship. But in that dreadful gaseous luminosity there was nothing, so far as I could see, that any mortal man could by any possibility be afraid of, alive or dead. So I left him to the porter. And – as yet – we have not met again.

Note on the text

These three stories are included in the three-volume edition of Walter de la Mare's stories, *Short Stories 1895–1926*, *Short Stories 1927–1956* and *Short Stories for Children*, all published by Giles de la Mare Publishers.

Biographical note

Walter de la Mare was born in Charlton, Kent, in 1873 and was educated at St Paul's Choir School in London. At sixteen, he went to work as a clerk in the statistics department of an oil company, a job in which he stayed for eighteen years until a government pension allowed him to concentrate solely on writing.

In his mid-twenties, de la Mare began to submit his work to various magazines and in 1902 his first collection of poems, *Songs of Childhood*, was published, under the name of Walter Ramal. He subsequently published sixteen volumes of poetry under his own name, including *The Listeners* (1912) and *The Veil* (1921) and for children, *Peacock Pie* (1913) and *Bells and Grass* (1941). His prose includes the novels *The Return* (1910) and *Memoirs of a Midget* (1921), which won the James Tait Black Memorial Prize for Fiction. De la Mare was also an accomplished short story writer, publishing eight collections including *The Riddle* (1925) and *The Lord Fish* (1933). His *Collected Stories for Children* (1947) was awarded the Carnegie Medal.

Walter de la Mare was made a Companion of Honour in 1948 and was given the Order of Merit in 1953. He died in Twickenham in 1956 and is buried in St Paul's Cathedral.

SELECTED TITLES FROM HESPERUS PRESS

Author	Title	Foreword writer
Mikhail Bulgakov	*A Dog's Heart*	A.S. Byatt
Mikhail Bulgakov	*The Fatal Eggs*	Doris Lessing
Anthony Burgess	*The Eve of St Venus*	
Colette	*Claudine's House*	Doris Lessing
Marie Ferranti	*The Princess of Mantua*	
Beppe Fenoglio	*A Private Affair*	Paul Bailey
F. Scott Fitzgerald	*The Popular Girl*	Helen Dunmore
F. Scott Fitzgerald	*The Rich Boy*	John Updike
Graham Greene	*No Man's Land*	David Lodge
Franz Kafka	*Metamorphosis*	Martin Jarvis
Franz Kafka	*The Trial*	Zadie Smith
D.H. Lawrence	*Wintry Peacock*	Amit Chaudhuri
Rosamond Lehmann	*The Gipsy's Baby*	Niall Griffiths
Carlo Levi	*Words are Stones*	Anita Desai
André Malraux	*The Way of the Kings*	Rachel Seiffert
Katherine Mansfield	*In a German Pension*	Linda Grant
Katherine Mansfield	*Prelude*	William Boyd
Vladimir Mayakovsky	*My Discovery of America*	Colum McCann
Luigi Pirandello	*Loveless Love*	
Françoise Sagan	*The Unmade Bed*	
Jean-Paul Sartre	*The Wall*	Justin Cartwright
Bernard Shaw	*The Adventures of the Black Girl in Her Search for God*	Colm Tóibín
Georges Simenon	*Three Crimes*	
Leonard Woolf	*A Tale Told by Moonlight*	Victoria Glendinning
Virginia Woolf	*Memoirs of a Novelist*	